Put My Name On It

By

Princess Diamond

Twitter & Instagram: @authorprincess
Facebook: @authorprincessdiamond
Pinterest: princess diamond

Put My Name On It

Dedication

I dedicate this book to all the authors who love to write and don't know where to begin. To all the authors who have been told no or received rejection letters. You can do it! I'm living proof. I did everything on my own. It is possible. Never give up. Blessings.

Acknowledgements

I give all praises to God who anointed me with this wonderful gift of writing. Through Christ I can do all things.

To my father in heaven, you passed away too soon. You never got to see any of my work, but I write in your memory. Love always.

To my family and friends, I couldn't have done this without your endless days of listening to me talk about my stories, offering ideas, and giving me advice. You all are my rock. Thanks for everything.

To my readers, without your support, there is no me. I appreciate you all.

XOXOX
Princess Diamond

Princess Diamond's Books

Element of Surprise

Element of Surprise 2: Lust Unleashed

Put My Name On It

Hott Girlz Series

Dream & Drake Series

Chapter 1

Cash hit the end button on his cell. "Karen said they'll be here in a minute."

"Yo, I'm really not trying to hear you right now." Marcel got off the stool at the breakfast bar, ready to leave.

He was at the door turning the knob when Cash blocked his path. "Would you calm the hell down? You look like you about to bolt through the door." He snickered at Marcel's urgency to leave. "I told you, I got you. Be easy."

"I'm not fuckin around with that shit no more. The last girl you hooked me up with didn't look nothing like her picture. I swear, that chick was a man."

Cash laughed so hard he started coughing uncontrollably. "Aight, I feel you on that." He stopped laughing momentarily to address Marcel's comment. "You might be right. She was ugly as hell. My bad."

"See!" Marcel said, getting hyped. "That's that bullshit. I'm not trying to be set up like that no more. Nah, son, I'm good."

"You made your point, but check it, this girl coming through is fine. Karen hooked you up, fa real. Shorty's right. I seen her."

"How long ago was that?" Marcel asked still feeling some kind of way about his blind date.

"The other day. I wanted to see her for myself."

Marcel turned up his lips. "Yeah, just like you saw the last one?"

"Ok, I ain't gonna lie. I didn't see her. I went by Karen's word. And now I know, I can't go by what the hell she say. She always trying to be nice and shit. Helping all these ugly hoes find a man."

The skeptical look on Marcel's face said it all. "Nah, son, I'm good. I'll find my own girl."

"How about you just hang around until they get here. If you don't like her, I'll make up an excuse for you to bounce, aight?"

Marcel cut his eyes at his boy. He couldn't believe Cash was pressuring him to date another one of Karen's desperate friends. All her friends were ugly. He didn't see this girl being any different. "All I'm saying is, if she ugly, I'm out. I don't care. I'm not being nice this time."

Marcel's outburst caused Cash to start another laughing fit.

"What's so damn funny?" Marcel was getting real agitated with Cash's constant laughter.

Holding onto the kitchen counter, Cash tried to catch his breath. "Man, the look on your face is priceless. You look scared shitless."

Marcel wanted to stay angry at his boy but he couldn't. Cash's laughter was contagious. He was laughing so hard it made Marcel start laughing too. Before long, they were both talking about the whole experience as if it was funny all along.

This is why Cash was Marcel's best friend. He understood him in a way that most people didn't. They met in high school a few weeks before Marcel became the famous R&B singer turned Pop Star, Urbane.

They hit it off instantly, like long lost brothers. Having so much in common and looking alike, people often questioned if they were actually kin.

Quite naturally, when Marcel made it big, he asked Cash to come be by his side, sharing his success. From rocking the stage to accompanying him in the studio to being on tour, Cash was a permanent fixture.

Cash might have been new in Marcel's life, but he was different from his friends back home. All his boys in New York wanted to do was hustle. He wasn't down with the street life. Being raised in a two parent household, he had the same views, ambition, and drive as Marcel. This is what made Cash an intricate part of Marcel's life. Not to mention his loyalty. Cash always had Marcel's back, even when everyone else didn't.

"Aye, you want a shot before they get here?" Cash asked holding up an unopened bottle of premium Tequila.

3

"You know I don't normally drink that, but I think I might need it this time," Marcel confessed.

"Yeeeeeeeah!" Cash jumped up like a rock star, playing an air guitar. "That's what I'm talking about. Getting nice up in this bitch."

Marcel shook his head and laughed at the silliness.

"Wait, don't down it yet." Cash held up his shot for a toast. "To fine ass women, joe."

Marcel chuckled nervously, toasting with Cash. "I don't know about all that, but if you say so." Their glasses clinked and he knocked his shot back.

Cash reassured him again that this girl was different from all the rest. She had things going for her, but Marcel still wasn't convinced. "I promise you, this girl might be the one."

Marcel nearly choked. "Get that shit outta here. Ain't no damn way."

"I'm telling you, she might be. Wait until you meet her."

Cash knew his boy had been single for months. It wasn't like he couldn't get a date on his own. He had women throwing pussy at him from East Coast to West Coast. However, those women weren't worth a pot to piss in.

Marcel was a good dude. Cash wanted a good woman for him. His last relationship ended abruptly. They'd been together for six years. Just when Marcel was about to pop the question, he found out she had been playing him, using him for his money and fame.

Without causing a scene, Marcel let her go and went on with his life as usual, throwing himself into his music. Cash knew his friend was hurt deeply by the break up. Although Marcel never verbally expressed it, they were tight like that. Cash automatically knew when Marcel was heartbroken.

"What will you do if she is cute?"

Marcel paused, thinking about the question carefully before he answered. "I'ma make her call me daddy."

Feeling nice off the Tequila, he stood to his feet doing one of his signature stripper dance moves. A sensual body roll that showed off his flexibility and hardrock abs. Ladies went crazy each time he did it, imagining that he worked his body the same way in the bedroom.

"Nah, make her call out your name. That's how I got Karen. I gave her the dick so good she had no choice but to say it. I had her sprung."

"No doubt. I'ma do better than that." Marcel used his finger as though it were a pen, pretending to write his name in cursive on her imaginary body. "I'ma put my name on it."

"My nicca." Cash knocked knuckles with Marcel. "I like that even better. I taught you well."

"Get the hell outta here. If anything I taught you. Who lost their virginity first?"

"You," Cash conceded. "With your nasty ass."

They chuckled.

Cash poured them another shot. "On a serious note, when do you start touring?"

"I'm not sure," Marcel answered truthfully. "Mia said it could be any day now. I wish you would reconsider being my assistant again. I can't even front, you were the best."

"I wish I could too," Cash replied honestly. "But the thing is I can't spend that much time away from Karen. I love her too much. You'll understand when you find that special woman. Being apart for long periods of time feels like torture."

"Nah, I get it," Marcel lied. *I hope he don't see the lie written all over my face.*

Marcel got that Karen made Cash very happy. What he didn't understanding was how his boy could pass up an opportunity of a lifetime for a woman.

Chapter 2

"Hold still," Karen said in frustration. She was putting Natalia's makeup on and she kept moving. "If you don't be still you're going to make me poke your damn eye out."

"Okaaaaay." Natalia sighed still feeling antsy. She had been sitting on top of the toilet so long that her ass was numb. Being in one spot for such a long period of time was harder than she thought. Wearing makeup wasn't her thing. Karen convinced her to try something new just like this blind date thing.

Natalia rolled her eyes. "I don't see what the big deal is. He's probably crazy anyway."

"Girl, you better stop moving!" Karen screamed, stomping her foot on the bathroom tile. Natalia's sudden movement almost messed up her eyeliner. "And what you talking about? All men ain't crazy. Just those knuckleheads you mess with."

Karen took offense to Natalia's insinuation because she knew Marcel personally. He was a good guy. She admits to hooking him up with a couple of her friends that weren't a good match. However, Natalia was perfect for him.

Doubtful, Natalia tried everything in her power to get out of this hook-up. It seemed like every man she met was totally wrong for her. She had little faith that this man would be any different. Besides, she met some of Cash's other friends. They were goofy, cheap, and had no class. She couldn't imagine Marcel being any different.

"All done." Karen stood back admiring her handiwork. "You look stunning."

Natalia stood up, looking in the mirror. She had to admit Karen did her thing. The makeup was flawless just like her hair in long tresses. "Girl, you did the damn thang."

"I know," Karen beamed. "Now finish getting ready so we can leave. We're late and Cash is blowing me up." She let all of his calls roll straight to voicemail. He didn't realize that calling her back to back was slowing her down even more.

The girls quickly fixed themselves up, hopped into Karen's car, and sped over to Cash's house. The men were standing on the porch when they pulled up.

Natalia checked Marcel out. She squinted trying to get a better look. *No, it can't be. This man looks just like Urbane. Am I seeing things?*

Marcel checked Natalia out too. "Damn, is that her? She's fly." He was instantly attracted to her the moment she stepped out the car.

"I told you," Cash replied, polishing off his vodka and cranberry. "I hope you ready to kick game."

"You better ask somebody. I was born ready."

Cash chuckled. "Ok, playboy." He was just glad his boy was finally excited about his date.

Marcel couldn't take his eyes off Natalia. He knew right away that she was his type—classy with a lot of sexy. He really liked the red sweater dress she had on accented with a black belt around her small waist and black thigh boots. Her face was painted with a hint of makeup and she wore a touch of jewelry.

"It took y'all asses long enough," Cash yelled as they approached. "What was the hold up?"

Karen ignored his question, giving him a hug. "Don't start. You know beauty takes time." She kissed him on the lips and squeezed his butt. "If you keep questioning me, I won't let you undress me later." She winked at him, letting him know that she had something freaky in mind. Not wanting to mess things up, Cash fell back, allowing Karen to do whatever she wanted.

"This is my best friend and cousin, Natalia." Karen pushed Natalia forward so that she was standing face to face with Marcel. "She's the one I told you about."

Up close and personal, Natalia saw that she wasn't tripping at all. Her blind date was Urbane. Trying to keep her cool, she batted her fake eyelashes, giving him a cute little wave. "Hey."

Tenderly taking Natalia's freshly manicured hand into his, Marcel raised it to his lips, kissing it. "Nice to meet you, beautiful." *Damn, she's hot.*

"Natalia, this is Cash's homeboy, Urbane."

Marcel barely noticed the cheesy grin on Karen's face because his eyes were glued to Natalia. "I'm just a regular guy. Call me, Marcel."

Wow, how did I get so lucky? "Nice to meet you too, Marcel," Natalia said bashfully, feeling like a groupie. On the outside she remained calm, but on the inside she was thinking, *Oh, shit. I got me a winner.* She couldn't believe that she was standing face to face with the famous R&B Singer. All his albums were multi-platinum. *I'ma kill Karen for keeping this secret from me.*

Karen smiled from ear to ear, pleased with her match making skills. *They look so cute together. They are going to get married and have a bunch of babies.*

Cash snapped his fingers, breaking up the inquisitive stares between Natalia and Marcel. "Hey, let's go. I'm hungry as hell."

Marcel looked away first. *She got me mesmerized. I gotta get myself together.* He walked off the porch in the direction of his car across the street.

Natalia followed behind Karen and Cash.

Karen stopped her in her tracks. "Where do you think you're going?" she whispered.

Put My Name On It

"With you," she mumbled.

"Uh-uhn, girl, you riding with him. You're on a date, remember?"

Natalia gave Karen a funky look. "No, I'm not," she said through clenched teeth. "I don't care if he is famous. I don't know him like that. Shoot, he might be crazy for real. He got enough money to make me disappear forever." She looked over her shoulder to see where Marcel was. Thankfully, he wasn't in earshot.

Karen grinned, but replied with the same clenched teeth response. "That's why you riding with him. So you can get to know him, groupie."

"I'm nobody's groupie."

Karen gave her a little nudge, pushing her in Marcel's direction. "Stop being so scary. Besides, you are a groupie. You got all seven albums. And you know all the damn lyrics. Quit playing and get up on that dick before the next chick do."

Cash stuck his head out the car window. "What's the problem, baby girl?" Natalia rolled her eyes at him. "I know you can walk faster than that. A brutha is hungry."

Marcel waited by the curb, silently laughing at the sour look on Natalia's face. He could tell she wanted to say something slick to Cash instead of keeping her composure.

Look at the sway of her hips, he thought, hypnotized by her seductive walk. *I bet she got some good pussy.*

He couldn't help but lick his lips in anticipation of what his dick would feel like inside her. Her demeanor told him that she was a good girl that hadn't found the right man yet. *Good looking, Cash. I gotta play my cards right with this one.*

The moment Natalia made it over to him, Marcel put his arm around her waist, resting his palm against the small of her back. They walked across the street towards his ride. He used the keyless remote to unlock the door to his brand new custom-made white Infiniti convertible. A gift he received from the label.

"After you," he said, opening the door for her.

"Thank you," she said, sliding onto the plush leather seat.

Marcel closed the door and swiftly walked around to the driver's side getting in.

She looked over at Karen who mouthed, *girl you better smile.*

Natalia plastered a smile on her face after flipping Karen the bird. She was putting up a fuss, but she was definitely impressed with Marcel so far. He wasn't the stuck up entertainer that she was used to meeting. Being filthy rich, she never would have expected him to act like the boy next door. She met quite a few local celebrities and found none of them appealing. If it wasn't the excessive money they tossed around, it was their god-like persona that turned her off.

Put My Name On It

"Anyone riding with me is required to wear a seat belt," Marcel said while putting his on. He wondered why Natalia didn't budge. Looking over at her, he noticed she was already clicked in. "I have to twist most people's arm to get them to buckle up."

"I'm not most people," she replied, avoiding his stare. "And you shouldn't assume. It makes an ass out of you. Besides, I never ride without one."

Marcel was really digging her. Obviously, she wasn't threatened by his status, which he found very appealing. He liked a woman who spoke her mind.

"Safety first," they said in unison.

Marcel cleared his throat choosing to ignore what just happened. Natalia did the same, pretending to look out the window. They might have met only moments ago, but the chemistry between them was undeniable.

Breaking the silence, Marcel said, "What kind of music you like?"

Natalia leaned over trying to see what he was holding in his hand. "What you got?"

Marcel wasn't sure what he had. He cleaned out his car the other day and most of the music was cleaned out too. He flipped through some local talent before he came across a classic. "How about some Jodeci?"

The first one?" He held it up for her to see that's what it was. "Yeah, that'll work."

"I love that CD," they said in unison again.

"Why you keep doing that?" Natalia asked him,

deciding not to ignore it this time.

Marcel was about to address her question when Cash honked his horn. "Y'all ready or what? Like I said, a brutha is starving like Marvin."

"Bring your slow ass on then," Marcel yelled out the window pressing down on the gas, taking off while Cash continued to complain. Marcel was turning the corner by the time Cash realized that he already pulled off.

Chapter 3

They drove to Sigel's Restaurant. It was a new joint that just opened. Most people said it was an upscale Olive Garden. Critics said the food was off the chain. It was getting rave reviews and quickly becoming the talk of the city.

Marcel approached the hostess asking if he could get a private cozy area for him and Natalia. As soon as they were seated in a secluded area, the waiter promptly took their order.

Marcel took the liberty of ordering for them both. "Crab cakes for an appetizer. The main dishes are Lobster Ravioli and Spaghetti and Meatballs. For desert, we'll have Chocolate Brownies and John Cole. And please bring us your best bottle of red wine." He handed the waiter the menu.

"Thank you, sir. I'll be right back." The waiter rushed away towards the kitchen. Within in seconds, he returned with the expensive bottle of wine, two glasses, and the crab cakes.

"Thank you," Marcel replied.

"You're quite welcome, sir. Is there anything else I can get for you?"

"No, thank you. That'll be all for now."

"The rest of your food will be ready shortly." The waiter walked away, disappearing into another section of the restaurant.

Marcel poured the wine into both glasses, handing one to Natalia. "Let's make a toast."

Natalia took her glass and frowned. "I can't believe you ordered for me. What if I didn't want that?"

"You'll like it," Marcel said in a cocky manner. "Now, let's toast to a new beginning."

Confused, Natalia asked, "What new beginning?"

"To us going half on a baby." Marcel laughed at his own joke, but Natalia didn't find it funny, giving him the stank face. He straightened up when he saw that she wasn't laughing. "Where's your sense of humor?"

"On your face, son!" Natalia said, imitating his hard New York accent, laughing loudly.

Marcel loosened up, smiling. "You got me with that one."

She struck a B-boy pose. "Word!"

"I see you real live right now." He chuckled at her theatrics. "That was cute. Real cute."

She stopped acting silly and raised her glass to his. "To new beginnings."

They toasted and took a sip before sitting the glasses on the fancy table covering.

"Have you eaten here before?" Marcel asked, honestly.

"Are you for real? This place is one day's pay for me," she openly admitted. "Have you?" *What a stupid ass question. Why did I ask him that? Of course, he has. He's rich enough to own the place.*

"Yes, quite a few times." He took another sip of wine and then stared deep into her eyes trying to figure her out. "So, tell me more about you."

She avoided his stare, taking a gulp of wine out of nervousness. "What do you want to know?"

"Everything," he said in a flirty manner. "Tell me what you do for fun."

"I like to do a variety of things—"

Marcel scooted closer to her. "A *variety* of what?" he asked, taking her hand in his.

Natalia wanted to tell him to back up, but it was something about him that intrigued her. She didn't want to admit it, but she liked the attention he was giving her. "Well, I like to dance, shop, and travel," she rattled off. "What about you?"

"I like to dance, shop, and travel too," Marcel said with his lips only inches from hers.

He was way too close. Normally, Natalia would have slapped fire from any man who did that to her on the first date, but Marcel had her wide open. She was digging his sexy style. His cologne was intoxicating. His eyes were inviting. His personality was contagious.

Marcel knew she was feeling him. Without hesitation, he seized the moment, leaning in to kiss her. Just as he thought, she didn't resist, allowing his lips to part hers. Gently touching her face, he gave her a tender French kiss.

Natalia relaxed her body against him as his hand moved up her thigh. When she didn't push him away, Marcel moved his hand under her dress. His fingers skillfully outlined her silk pearl through her thong.

Natalia amazed herself when she opened her legs wider, enjoying his kiss and the feel of his fingers between her legs.

As turned on as she was, she thought about letting him hit it right then and there. He brought out the freak in her. Thoughts of lying across the table spreading her legs open crossed her mind.

Marcel put her hand down his pants so she could feel his growing erection. "See what you do to me?"

Natalia gasped in heat as he sucked on her bottom lip. *Mmmmm. He feels real big.* The size of his manhood scared her and excited her at the same time. *I wonder what he feels like inside of me.*

Marcel was all over her. He was ready to rip both their clothes off. He might have done just that if the waiter hadn't returned asking if they needed anything else. The interruption promptly brought them back to reality.

Marcel stopped kissing her. *This dude couldn't have come back at a worse time.* "No. We're fine."

"Yes, sir. Just making sure, sir," the waiter stammered before he quickly disappeared.

Marcel focused his attention back on Natalia, leaning over, kissing her neck.

As much as Natalia liked how Marcel made her feel, she couldn't get back in the groove. She was embarrassed feeling more like a groupie than his date for the evening. The smug look on the waiter's face made her feel dirty and ashamed. He stared at her with disdain. She was sure when he left that he told the rest of the staff how trifling she was.

"Stop." Natalia lightly pushed Marcel way, avoiding his attempt to kiss her again. "I can't do this."

"You can't? Why? What happened?"

"Nothing," Natalia said, feeling her face getting flush. "I just want you to stop. That's all."

At Natalia's request, Marcel chilled out. He sighed with aggravation displaying his apparent frustration. "Something must've happened for you to switch things up."

She looked away adjusting her dress. Allowing him to feel her up definitely gave him the wrong impression.

"Aren't you going to say something?"

Natalia was still in her feelings. She couldn't believe she allowed Marcel to get her in such a compromising position, especially out in public. This was way out of her character. She wasn't easy by no means. This incident made him look at her like another piece of ass instead of a woman with class.

"You were just into it a few seconds ago." Marcel looked Natalia over waiting for her to respond.

She didn't even attempt to answer him, making it evident that they wouldn't finish what they started, like he hoped.

Food wasn't on Marcel's mind anymore. All he wanted was to slide between Natalia's warm thighs, but her demeanor indicated that the mood had changed. In fact, she looked completely turned off, ready to run away from the table.

Abruptly, Marcel stood. "I'll be back." He practically stomped away. He had to get away from her. Sitting at that table one more minute would have caused a scene. Cuss words were on the tip of his tongue.

Walking briskly, Marcel couldn't get to the bathroom quick enough. He raced into one of the empty stalls slamming the door, leaning back against it. Angry as hell, he balled up his fists squeezing them tight before taking a few deep breaths. Blowing up wasn't the best choice so he contemplated what to do next.

Having a hard dick had him all messed up. He couldn't think clearly because his imagination was running rapid. Wanting to give into his anger, he thought about going back to their table, calling her all kinds of foul names, embarrassing her.

Put My Name On It

Why am I trippin over this girl? I must be slippin. I just met her and she got me in the bathroom thinking things over like I'm a bitch. If anything I should have dismissed her ass. I'm the one paying. Besides, I've dated some of the most beautiful women in the world. And I've fucked some of the industries finest. How dare she treat me like I'm nobody? Plenty of bitches want to keep me company.

Marcel was so angry he began to sweat.

She was a dick tease. She needs to be called out on it. Getting me all worked up. Then expecting me to stop just because she said so. Things didn't work that way. She can't turn me on and off like a light switch. She don't know how I do. If a woman I just met treated me like she did, I would drop a few bills on the table and roll out on her ass and go get pussy elsewhere.

While Marcel was deep in thought, he heard two pair of feet enter the restroom. Swiftly, he stood on the toilet so he wouldn't be seen.

"He must've kicked cutie pie to the curb," a voice with a powerful lisp said. "Chile, she is looking too sad and pitiful." He giggled like a school girl. "And I don't blame her either, hunnie. I'd be ready to cry too if I lost a handsome baller like that."

"I'm sure he did," a familiar voice said. It sounded like their waiter. "What did she expect? Homie didn't ask her out because he thought she was cute. He just wanted some ass. Dudes like him get dozens of pretty girls all the time. She gotta put out to stay in his presence."

"He didn't have to do Little Miss Cutie Pie like that though. She seemed like such a sweet girl. If all he wanted was a hot piece, he shouldn't have picked a good girl." He smacked his lips. "See, that's why I needs me a real man. I don't have time to be playing no games. Giving away my goodies just to get dumped." He sucked in air again, making an irritating sound for a dramatic effect. "I bet Miss Thang was too embarrassed when you walked up."

"She should have been. Her dress was practically around her neck. I'm sure if I hadn't walked up when I did, he would have fucked her right then and there. I know I would have. I'm thinking about asking her out. Maybe I can hit that tonight."

Marcel was disgusted listening to their conversation. He wanted to rush out the stall and beat the dog shit out of both of them. However, as much as he wanted to get mad at them, he couldn't. Actually, it was all his fault. He put Natalia in this predicament.

And that's when things got weird. After the waiter came to our table. Her silence wasn't disrespect like I thought. It was shame. Why didn't I notice that? Man, I feel like such a jerk right now.

Bolting out the bathroom stall, Marcel expected to bump into the two men that were talking. Instead, all he saw was a reflection of himself. They were long gone.

They left while he was replaying the incident over again in his mind.

He exited the bathroom in a flash, making his way back to their table only to find Natalia gone. For some reason he expected to see her sitting there waiting for him to return.

This shit is all my fault. I gotta find her and make things right.

Chapter 4

Natalia couldn't believe Marcel walked off. Her feelings were crushed. She had high hopes of getting to know him. Thinking about what went wrong made her want to cry. She let her guard down with regret.

I was all wrong about him. I thought he was differ-ent. I guess not. He fooled me. He's just like all the other industry men.

She was hurt because she really liked him. Things between them felt so right. A chemistry that she never felt before. Like they were destined to meet each other, and possibly be together forever.

Silently, she blamed herself for the turn of events. She realized that she led him on. If she hadn't given him the wrong impression, he wouldn't be so upset with her. In fact, they'd be sitting cozy at their private table conversing over dinner instead of being in two different parts of the restaurant.

After waiting a few minutes for Marcel to return, she finally got up from the table, walking away. Every-one appeared to be staring at her as she made her way to the front door.

Put My Name On It

Is my mind playing tricks on me?

She wondered if she was just being paranoid or if the whole restaurant knew what happened between her and Marcel.

Ignoring the stares, she approached two male greeters by the entrance. "Excuse me, do you think you can call me a cab?"

"Yeah sure," the younger one said, staring at her, making her feel really cheap before he walked away.

If she didn't know any better, she would have thought he knew what just happened. Then again, this was a restaurant. News traveled fast. She was sure that most of the staff was talking about how she just degraded herself.

The greeter returned. "You're cab is on the way, Miss," he said, politely. Although, she could see the judgment in his eyes.

Feeling very uneasy, Natalia took a seat in the waiting area. She would have made herself invisible if she could have. With the back of her hand, she quickly wiped away the tears threatening to fall. Her gaze stayed plastered to the floor avoiding all eye contact until someone said her cab was outside. She thanked whoever announced the arrival without looking in their direction and then exited the restaurant in shame. Sitting in the backseat of the cab's confines, she allowed a few tears to fall.

"Where you going, sweetheart?" the overweight

cab driver asked her with an Italian accent.

"She's not going anywhere," Marcel said, yanking the cab door open, leaning inside.

The cabbie looked at Natalia for an answer. "You know this man, sweetheart?"

"Yes," Natalia admitted.

Marcel pulled out a hundred, slapping it in the cabbie's palm. "Thanks for your services. You can leave now." Carefully, he reached into the cab pulling Natalia out.

The cabbie waited for a response from Natalia, but she was out of the cab before he could hear her reply. He studied the two before pocketing the crisp bill, driving to his next destination.

Marcel stared deep into Natalia's eyes with his lips near hers. When she didn't pull away, he leaned down, kissing her softly.

Natalia put her arms around his neck, enjoying the kiss temporarily before pushing him away. "If all you want is sex I'm calling another cab."

She turned to walk away and Marcel pulled her back to him. Her backside against his groin. "Don't leave."

"Why not?" she asked, loving the way his strong hands held her small waist. "Why should I stay?"

Marcel nibbled on her ear and then whispered, "Because you like me." Natalia tried to protest, but he shut her down when he kissed her neck. "Nothing to be

26

ashamed about. I like you too."

Natalia tried to pull away from him. And he pulled her right back to him. "Quit fighting. This is where you belong. With me."

"Is that right?"

"Yes, love, it is." Marcel kissed her face as she squirmed under his touch.

He stirred feelings inside of her that she thought were dead. Being in his arms felt way too natural. *It's like he knows me. Like we've dated before. How could this be when we just met? What is going on?*

Marcel twirled her around so she was facing him. "Forgive me?"

"What?" Natalia was caught totally off guard.

"Forgive me?" Marcel repeated lovingly.

She closed her eyes and took a deep breath. "I forgive you." The three words rolled off her tongue in a whisper. "It's not your fault. I should have never let it go that far."

"Don't blame yourself for my mistake." Marcel stroked her cheek so she would open her eyes and look at him. "I take full responsibility for what happened earlier. I should have never treated you that way. I was hoping that maybe we could start over?'

"I don't know, Marcel. I don't think you're the man I'm looking for."

"Yes, I am. You just don't know it yet."

Natalia rolled her eyes. "Let me rephrase it. I'm

not putting out and it seems like that's what you're after."

"Actually, I'm not." Natalia gave him a disbelieving look. "Well, what I mean is, I want that from you, but I want to get to know you too. I'm not looking for just one night with you. I'm looking to spend time with you too."

"I still don't think we're on the same page."

"Please." Marcel couldn't believe he was outside begging her to give him another chance. Before his ego could kick in again, he quickly humbled himself. "I'll be on my best behavior." Natalia still didn't look convinced. "Can I be honest with you?"

"I'm listening."

"When Cash told me that Karen wanted to hook me up with someone, I wasn't expecting to get you. I had preconceived notions about how tonight would go. In my mind I thought you would be just a booty call."

Natalia processed what he said and decided to come clean too. "I can admit that I had my mind made up too. I thought you were going to be crazy."

Marcel chuckled. "You thought I was crazy?"

Natalia laughed with him. "I guess I owe you an apology, huh?"

"Look, it's obvious that we have mad chemistry. I'm feeling you and you're feeling me. It has to be true because we can't keep our hands off each other."

Natalia grinned.

"I'll admit, I am attracted to you. But right now all I want is dinner."

"Just dinner?"

"Yes, just dinner. Nothing else."

"Promise?"

"I promise." Marcel said before he tongued her down again.

"If you keep doing that, I'm going to cancel."

"Why? Because you like it?"

Natalia playfully hit him. "Maybe."

"Stop frontin. You like it." He flashed a sexy grin. "Nah, but fa real, I want to get to know you over dinner if that's ok with you?"

Her eyes danced with his for a moment before she answered. "Ok, lead the way."

Natalia followed Marcel back inside. Hand in hand, she couldn't help but feel vindicated from all the funny looks and whispers she got not too long ago when people thought she was kicked to the curb. It felt good knowing that she didn't go out foul like they thought she did.

She smiled even more when Marcel asked to speak to the manager, telling him about the mistreatment towards her from the staff and demanded another table and a new waiter. The manager reacted swiftly, accommodating Marcel's request.

Over dinner, Marcel and Natalia found out they had a lot in common. Their similarities were an ice breaker, allowing them both to let their guards down and loosen up. They realized they were the same age, twenty-five. They had the same favorite color, white. They liked the same travel spot, Jamaica. And when they were younger, they both broke the same arm in the same year. The more they talked, the more they realized how similar their lives were.

"I never expressed this to anyone before, but I feel so comfortable with you. Growing up, I was really shy. And even though I'm from Harlem, I was fortunate to be sheltered from the mean streets of New York. My boys back home always say that I'm not New York enough."

Marcel chuckled as he reminisced. "I know they're just joking, but in a funny kinda way, they're right. Because out of all of them, I'm the only one who hasn't hustled or been to jail."

"How did you keep things so straight? I mean if that was all around you, how did you avoid it?"

"I stayed in the crib a lot until I moved here to Chicago. When I was fifteen, I reconnected with my father. He asked me to come live with him so we could work on our relationship. Surprisingly, I said yes. It was the best decision of my life. I gained so much confidence from mending my relationship with him. When he found out I could sing, he encouraged me to perform everywhere. And six months later, I was discovered in a local talent show. The is rest history."

"That's a classic rags to riches story."

"Yeah, I guess it is. After a successful career as a multiplatinum artist, I wanted to help other artists. So I started my own record label."

Natalia liked the fact that Marcel was so down to earth. "Tell me something I wouldn't guess about you?"

"I'll tell you two things. I go to church as much as I can. My faith keeps me grounded. The second thing is I have two charities dedicated to helping urban youth."

She smiled widely with admiration. "I'm impressed." Hearing him openly admit how important his faith was impressed her the most. Although, she was quite amazed with his philanthropy too.

"Enough about me. I want to know more about you," Marcel said, giving her his undivided attention.

Natalia took a deep breath. Just like him, she didn't like opening up too soon. "Well, I used to have a high powered job with the Chicago Stock Exchange."

"Word?" Marcel was thoroughly impressed.

Natalia giggled. "Yes."

Marcel smiled with amazement. "Brains and beauty. I like that."

Natalia beamed. It always felt good when a man recognized her for more than her looks. "Yeah, I'm a broker. I got this amazing opportunity right after high school to join a stock program. It taught me the ins-and-outs of the business. Within two years, I was a broker. My technique was so phenomenal that I was recruited to work at the Chicago Stock Exchange."

"Wow! Now, that's real impressive."

Natalia blushed. "Stop it." She giggled a little and then she stopped abruptly, becoming very serious. "Anyway, both my parents became very ill."

"Hold up, both your parents got sick at the same time?"

"Yeah, as strange as it sounds, I found myself struggling with two really sick parents at the same time. It was crazy because one minute they were both fine and then my mother got sick. My father followed shortly after. I was thrown into being the sole caregiver for them. And—"

"That's why you decided to go into nursing," he said, finishing her sentence. "It makes sense."

Talking about her parents was a touchy subject. It always made her sad. Masking her true feelings, she continued, "I'm working for a home health agency while I finish up my nursing degree. I don't have that much longer before I'll be registered."

"Sounds like you've got it all figured out." Marcel like the fact that she cared for her parents. He always put a strong emphasis on family. He was glad she did too. "Now, it's your turn."

Natalia still in her feelings about the death of her parents instantly became defensive. "My turn for what?"

"To tell me something I wouldn't guess about you."

Marcel's grin lightened her mood. "Hold up, how you gonna do what I did?"

Marcel smiled sheepishly. "Hey, all is fair in love and war."

"Is this love or war?" Natalia flirted.

"Nice try. Don't change the subject. Answer the question."

Natalia liked the fact that he was quick on his feet. "I guess you'd be surprised that I've only had one boyfriend."

"Get the hell outta here." Marcel threw his napkin at her for emphasis.

"No, it's true. We met in high school. He was my first love. My first sexual experience. My first everything." Natalia slowly exhaled. She didn't want to get emotional reminiscing about him. "I thought it was the end of the world when he cheated on me. It broke my heart to pieces. I loved that man with everything that I had."

Marcel felt her heartache. He reached over, holding her hand for support. "How long ago was that?"

"A year ago," Natalia exclaimed, wiping tears away. "I've been single every since. Well, until now. No pressure, of course."

"No pressure taken." Marcel liked her even more. "Does that mean no sex either?"

Princess Diamond

She lowered her eyes painfully admitting yes by nodding her head.

He took Natalia into his arms, comforting her. It was evident that speaking about her ex really affected her. "Yo, your ex was an ass. Any man that would throw away years like that definitely ain't worth your time."

Natalia looked up at him with teary eyes. "Thank you."

Marcel understood her more. This is why she was so quick to leave. She probably thought he was a hoe ass nicca just like her ex.

"Well, let me clear something up. I'm not that dude. I would never do a woman that way. If it's just sex, I make it known. If it's something more, I say that too. I try to be as direct as I can. Besides, if you were still with him, you wouldn't have met me."

Natalia sat up straight, sniffling. She took the same cloth napkin that he threw at her, tossing it back at him. "Don't get full of yourself."

"Nah, never that. But seriously, I know how you feel. My ex was a bitch. I don't like calling women that, but she was in every sense. All she loved was my money. Just like you, I wanted to take things to the next level when I found out she was doing me dirty. But shit happens, right?"

"All the damn time," she said, checking her makeup in the mirror.

34

Put My Name On It

They cuddled in silence for a few minutes, taking a moment for the deep rooted pain that they both shared.

"Let's make another toast," Marcel said, pouring more wine in both of their glasses. He held his glass in the air next to hers. "To shit happens."

"To shit happens." Her glass clinked against his. Natalia giggled and shook her head at his toast.

"What?" he asked, chuckling with her.

"You crazy, you know that?"

"And this is coming from a woman who called a cab in the middle of dinner?"

"Point taken."

"Did you have a good time? Be honest."

Natalia stared at him for a moment. "I did."

"Me too."

Chapter 5

After dinner, they made their way back to Cash's house, playing a few games. The guys were against the girls. Natalia and Karen kept losing no matter how hard they tried. They suspected the men of cheating since they kept beating the socks off them.

Tired of losing, the girls decided to quit. Karen got upset and stormed off towards the bedroom. Cash snickered, quickly following behind her.

Natalia glanced over at Marcel realizing that they were alone once again. Not trusting herself, she made up a lame excuse to get away from him, disappearing into the kitchen to get a bottled water.

Putting distance between them was her attempt to control the situation before it got out of hand. After having several glasses of wine, there was no way she could deny the intense attraction she felt towards him.

Opening the refrigerator, she noticed that the bottled water was on the bottom shelf, way in the back. That meant she had to practically climb in to get it. *Oh my goodness. I'm too tipsy for all this. I should have just gotten a glass of water.*

Put My Name On It

Marcel watched Natalia stroll out the room. He thought she was going to the bathroom. After a few minutes passed, he wondered what was taking her so long. Getting up from the couch, he began walking to the bathroom when he saw her in the kitchen bent over. Seeing her ass in the air made him lose the little bit of self-control he had left. All he could focus on was the swelling in his pants. Thinking with his other *head*, he walked up behind her positioning his manhood against her backside. "Let me help you."

Startled, Natalia jumped falling backwards into Marcel's arms. He locked his arms around her so when she tried to move, she couldn't slip away.

"Mmmmm," he moaned, planting soft kisses on the back of her neck.

"What are you doing?" she asked, trying to break away from his grasp.

"Shhhh," he whispered, nibbling on her neck. "Quit resisting me."

Stuck in between the refrigerator and Marcel, Natalia had nowhere to go. Marcel used this as leverage. She had been trying to get away from him all night. She succeeded previously, but not this time. He wanted her. And he had no doubt that she wanted him too. Still kissing her neck, he lifted her sweater dress until it rested on her wide hips, exposing her thong.

From the mixture of Marcel's hot touch and the coolness from the refrigerator, it was enough to drive her crazy. Trying to be strong, she resisted again. "Noooo, Marcel. We can't."

"Yeeeees, we can," Marcel told her, spinning her around to face him. As usual, her eyes avoided his. "Look at me," he demanded.

Her eyes instantly met his and before she could look away again, he asked. "Did you feel that?" He knew she did, but he wanted to hear her say it.

Natalia knew exactly what he was talking about. He was referring to the magnetic chemistry that emerged every time they came near each other.

"Yes," she finally admitted. "I feel it."

He placed his hand inside her thong, caressing her engorged clit. "Tell me to stop and I'll stop," he whispered.

Natalia wanted to tell him so bad. She couldn't form the words. It took everything in her to say no the last time.

Smiling, he knew she wouldn't say it. It was clear that she was equally attracted to him. Taking the lead, Marcel gently pushed Natalia back so that she rested against the kitchen counter. He parted her legs slightly so he had better access to please her.

Playing with her pearl, he asked her once again. "Tell me you don't like how this feels?" He moved in even closer. His fresh breath grazed her cheek as he spoke. "Do you want it?"

Put My Name On It

Lust consumed Natalia, just like it consumed him. She wanted Marcel in the worse way. Grabbing the back of his neck, she kissed him with intensity. "Yes, give it to me."

They were posted up in the kitchen, kissing and dry humping against each other. Ready to fuck right there in Cash's kitchen.

"I wondered where you two went—" Cash said, walking in on their passionate make out session.

Totally caught off guard, Marcel removed his hand from between Natalia's thighs, quickly stepping away from her. His face was flush from embarrassment. She held her head down in shame while tugging at her dress.

"My bad," Cash said, sincerely. "I had no idea. Don't mind me. I just came for some ice." He quickly went into the freezer, grabbing an ice tray. "Carry on," he said swiftly walking out as fast as he came in.

"This ain't gonna work," Natalia said, feeling sexually frustrated.

Marcel adjusted his clothes. "I agree. Let me take you home."

"Ok," she quickly agreed.

Chapter 6

On the ride to Natalia's house, they were both quiet, deep in thought. Multiple things ran through Marcel's mind. He was sure she was having second thoughts. *I pray she don't change her mind before we arrive.*

Natalia sat next to him, wondering if she was giving it up too soon. Yes, she wanted him. But one night stands really weren't her thing. She was a relationship type of chick with a 90-day rule. Besides, she liked him. She didn't want him to lose respect for her.

The moment Marcel pulled into Natalia's driveway, she told him thanks, getting out the car before he could respond. She was hoping to get inside without having to face him. That way her body wouldn't betray her. With her key in her hand, she walked briskly across the manicured lawn to the front door, opening it on the first attempt.

She was almost inside and about the close the door when Marcel slid through. "I know you didn't think you were getting away from me that easy." He spun her around, pushing her against the front door. Enjoying their kiss once again, they fell right back into the same groove as if no time had been lost.

Something about her made Marcel sniff after her like a dog in heat. She could have rejected him a million times and he'd still come back a million more. Deep down inside he knew that she felt the same way.

"We shouldn't," Natalia said, still trying to fight the urge.

"Why shouldn't we?" Marcel continued to feel her up. He hoped that his touch was wearing her down.

"Because you can't just fuck me and leave me like some thirsty bitch. You and I both know that if you get some right now, I might not ever see you again."

Marcel understood what she meant. He had no intentions of treating her that way. He liked her. "That's not true. I want more than sex from you. I was hoping you would let me take you out again tomorrow, if you're free."

Natalia closed her eyes so she could think straight. Staring into his handsome face was clouding her judgment. "Please, don't lead me on. My heart can't take it."

"I'm not. I'm definitely open to the possibility of where things might go with us."

She opened her eyes, searching his for the truth. Listening to her heart, she agreed. She felt that he was telling her the truth. Besides, she liked him too. And she was open to the possibility of getting to know him as well. "You promise." She poked her finger at his chest. "Don't run game on me either."

He took her hand and placed it on his fast beating heart. "Do you feel that?" She nodded yes. "That's how I felt when I first saw you."

"And how do I know that's not from lust?"

"You don't. But you'll never find out if you don't give us a chance."

Natalia glared at him, contemplating whether she should give in or not. Sensing how uneasy she was about the situation, Marcel wanted to reassure her. Yes, he was thinking with his other *head* again, but he meant every word that he said. "Having sex with you wouldn't change how I feel. I'm into you already. I have every intention of seeing you again, but that's totally up to you."

"I still don't know."

"Let me change your mind." Kneeling before her, he pulled her thong to the side, burying his face inside her fleshy folds, tasting her surpy juices. The sweet smile on Natalia's face was reassurance to Marcel that he made the right decision.

Lately, he'd been all work and no play. Finally, he was enjoying life. Work was the farthest thing from his mind at the moment.

Natalia bit her bottom lip when Marcel lifted her leg over his shoulder. The feeling of his wet tongue against her engorged clit nearly made her knees buckle.

Put My Name On It

He was driving her wild, sucking on her as if she were a T-bone steak. Closing her eyes, she felt chills. Electricity shot through her entire body making her cum with great force.

"Yeeeeesssssss!" Natalia screamed holding Marcel's head steady as she squirted in his mouth. Her orgasm was so strong that she had to hold onto him just to keep her balance.

Marcel stood to his feet knowing that he accomplished what he set out to do. A sly grin appeared on his face when he saw Natalia spent, resting against the door. Usually, he would have had her on her knees returning the favor, but his erection was pushing against his jeans. He couldn't wait another minute.

Lifting her left leg over his hip, he tried to penetrate her. As wet as she was, it still took him three attempts before he slid inside her tight hole. She wasn't a virgin, but she felt like one. He nearly nutted as soon as he entered her.

The powerful feeling had Marcel under her spell. He'd been intimate with many women, but none of them made him feel the way Natalia did. Her sugary walls squeezed on his dick like a vacuum. Each time he pulled out, it felt like his dick was being sucked right back in.

Oooooh, I knew she had some good pussy. My dick fits perfect. Damn I want to cum, but I can't go out like that. I have to concentrate on something.

43

Princess Diamond

Natalia immediately came back to life when he penetrated her. She began to roll her hips in sync with his hard thrusts. Her lips found his welcoming his tongue again. She rubbed her harden nipples against his chest. Her arms locked around his neck while she worked on her second orgasm.

She was on a mission. It showed from her wild and crazy movements. Humping and working her pussy on him like a dancer on a pole. Dipping it. Dropping it. Popping it. Doing it. She worked her pussy muscles in a way that she never knew she could. Rocking back and forth, she left unforgettable memories in Marcel's mind.

Slamming her up against the door in a passionate rage, he lifted her other leg for deeper penetration. He needed to feel her bounce on him when he finally let loose.

At that moment Natalia felt like she was going insane. Marcel hit her G spot every time he thrust deep inside of her. It was the best feeling. She wanted to stay in that moment forever. The intensity was overwhelming. The more she held back, the more intense the feeling became.

"Aaaah! Aaaah! Aaaah! Mar—" Her eyes rolled into the back of her head. She wanted to scream at the top of her lungs, but she couldn't say another word. That's how great it felt. His sex was so damn on point that she nearly choked on her own saliva trying to speak. Finally able to speak, she whispered, "I swear, you got the best dick in the world."

After Natalia came, her kitty cat was extra gushy. The wetness along with her warm breath on his ear and neck pushed him over the edge. He couldn't hold on any longer. Suppressing the emotion to yell out in ecstasy, he squeezed her ass while sucking on her neck. His body quivered mercilessly as he squirted inside of her like warm milk. Weak in the knees, Marcel dropped her legs and stepped back preparing to leave.

"You're leaving?" Natalia panted, still out of breath from their sex session.

"Yes, unless you want me to stay."

She stepped into his personal space, kissing his full lips. "Of course, I want you to stay. I was hoping we could do it again." She held his sexy gaze. "That's if you're up to it."

"You want some more of this, huh?" he asked her with lust-filled eyes. "Are you sure you can handle more of this?"

"Are you sure you can handle more of this?" Natalia fired back. She playfully turned around smacking her ass as she walked towards the steps. Intentionally bending over touching her toes, she showed off her flexibility. In perfect form, she gripped her ankles, unzipping her boots before stepping out of them. Walking up the stairs slow and sexy, she put extra emphasis in her stride giving her hips a very sensual sway.

Marcel watched from a far as she enticed him. His dick sprung to life again, throbbing, letting him know that he wanted more too. Within moments, he was right behind her gripping her by the hips, resting his erection against her backside. "You thought that shit was cute?"

Natalia giggled. "I don't know what you're talking about," she said, feigning ignorance.

"Let me show you how cute that was." He pulled her dress up over her ass penetrating her again. He plunged so deep that Natalia fell face first on the steps, landing on all fours. Marcel went to work on her pussy pounding her hard and fast.

"Ooooooh!" Natalia moaned. Marcel was hitting it so raw that she had to hold her breasts so that she didn't get a rug burn. "That's my spot. Ohmigod! Ohmigod! That's my spot." Natalia arched her back, matching him thrust for thrust. "Get it. Work that dick. Wooooooork...it..."

He was fucking her so good she had to turn around and look at him. Reaching behind with her free hand, she rested her palm against his stomach as he drove deeper and deeper into her. "Ah...Marcel... I'm...about...to...cummmm—"

Marcel rapidly jerked her hips towards him over and over again until she finally let out a piercing scream. Natalia yelled loud enough to wake every neighbor on the block before she collapsed on the steps.

Put My Name On It

"Urgh! Urgh! Urgh! Shiiiiiiiiiiit!" Marcel grunted while holding her hips steady, letting out another hot load deep inside of her.

Natalia lay across the steps breathing heavy from her third orgasm.

Marcel stood behind her with his eyes closed, enjoying the moment. He withdrew from her, wiping the sweat from his face. "You tired?"

Natalia was sprawled out on the carpet steps, drained.

Marcel was energized. "Meet me in the shower." He smacked her hard on the ass, walking pass her, upstairs. "And don't take all day." *I'ma beat that pretty pussy up. I haven't put my name on it yet.*

Wow, he got stamina! Natalia watched him walk up a few steps tugging at his pants before pulling them over his rear, jogging upstairs. *Nice ass!*

Chapter 7

Retreating to the shower, they washed each other's bodies and then retired to the bedroom.

Natalia crawled into the bed, curling up with her pillow, about to go to sleep.

Marcel crawled up behind her, spooning her. "You going to sleep?" he asked knowing that she was exhausted.

"Yes," she replied with her eyes closed. "Aren't you?"

"No," he said, feeling horny again. "I want some more." *I think I'm hooked*, he thought. *I can't get enough.*

"Whaaat?" Natalia squealed. "You can't be serious."

"Oh, but I am," he said, flipping her over onto her back. He climbed on top of her, sliding between her legs. "Just lay here and let me do all the work."

She looked up at him and smiled. "Addicted, huh?"

He kissed her soft lips and smiled. "Yep. Just like you a-dicked too."

Natalia didn't deny it. She was definitely hooked on him. His skills were incredible. She pulled him closer so that their bodies were intertwined.

Marcel wasn't in heat like he was earlier. He wanted to slow things down, making sweet love between the sheets. His moves were deliberately slow and sensual, enjoying every part of her body. His task was to leave a dick stamp on her pussy so that she would never forget him.

Taking his time, he kissed her face, neck and shoulders. After sucking on her breasts, he whispered sweet nothings in her ear, savoring every stroke.

"Is it good?" he asked.

"Uh-huh," she moaned.

He grabbed her by her wrists, stretching her arms over her head. "I want to hear you say it," he whispered seductively. "Tell me."

"No," Natalia playfully responded.

"No?" he questioned.

"No," she said again, giggling. "It might go to your head."

"I'm offended," Marcel joked. "Since you don't like it, I might as well stop."

Just like that Marcel quit rocking back and forth on top of her, pulling out.

"No!" Natalia screamed, feeling his penis against the hot flesh of her inner thigh. "Put it back in," she begged.

"Tell me you want it?" Marcel demanded, still lying on top of her, holding her wrists.

She wiggled under him, trying to flip him onto his back so she could ride him.

"Stop!" he said, pinning her down.

"No!" Natalia shrieked.

"Say it, then."

Natalia looked up at him. She studied his handsome face, smiling. "Ooooh, Marcel. Give it to me. It's sooooo good."

"You want it bad?"

"Yesssss," Natalia purred, feeling the tip of his penis at the opening of her vagina.

"How bad?"

"Bad enough," she replied, batting her long eyelashes.

Marcel made her grovel a little bit more before he slowly entered her again.

Natalia didn't think sex with Marcel could get any better until now. She raised her legs and locked them behind his back, rocking to the same relaxed rhythm.

Speaking in their own sexual language, they kissed, moaned, and explored each other's bodies until they climaxed at the same time. The passionate feeling started in their loins and erupted throughout both of their bodies, relieving them of all sexual tension.

"That was awesome," Marcel admitted.

"Yes, it was," Natalia agreed. "The best I ever had."

Marcel chuckled. "Look who's a-dicked now."

Natalia grinned. "I can't help it. Your sex is the bomb. I've never felt anything like it."

"Music to my ears." He looked down at her, wanting to confess how he felt too. He wondered if what he felt was only because of good sex. Or could it be something more? Something about being with her had him feeling so in tune with his emotions. He was definitely living in a moment with her.

I could stay like this forever. I'm so in love. What the hell am I saying? I can't be in love. Could I? Nah, I just met her. I'm wildin out. He shook off the idea, feeling even more confused.

Natalia stopped smiling when his expression changed. "Why are you looking at me like that? Something wrong?"

"It's nothing," he said trying to figure out why he suddenly felt the way that he did.

"Ok." Natalia wrapped her arms around him, holding him tight. "Good night."

"Good night." Marcel pecked her lips once more before he collapsed on top of her, resting his semi-hard dick comfortably inside of her vaginal walls.

Chapter 8

Marcel's phone woke him up. He was snuggled up next to Natalia dreaming of the love making from the night before when his cell rang. It kept ringing and vibrating until he finally snatched it off the floor, checking it. He had several missed calls and messages. After checking his voicemail, he realized that he was supposed to be at the office. He was so caught up in getting his dick wet that he totally forgot about this morning meeting.

Easing out of her bed, he put his clothes back on and walked around to the other side where Natalia was out cold. He gazed down at her thinking how beautiful she was as she slept. Removing a few strands of hair from her face, he leaned over kissing her cheek.

"I'm really into you that's why I had that look on my face. You make me feel things I never felt before. I didn't say it last night because I wasn't sure how you truly felt about me. I'm not trying to play myself, nahmean?" He chuckled when she didn't budge. *I must've really worn her ass out. She didn't even move.*

He had to admit, he was very tired too after having sex half the night. If he hadn't gotten that call, he would have stayed in bed curled up next to her soft body. The last thing he wanted to do was leave her side in such a hurry.

Waking her up wasn't an option. She looked so peaceful. He could tell that she needed her rest so he decided to let her be.

Standing by the bedside, he looked around the room for paper to write her a note. Of course, there wasn't any. Just as he was about to walk across the room to look for something else to write on, his phone rang again. Knowing that he needed to get to the office ASAP, he decided to leave.

I'll call her later and explain my disappearance. As soon as I take care of business.

Natalia woke up to the sun shining in her face. Her body was drained and a little sore from having marathon sex. Still, she couldn't help but smile when she thought about how Marcel put it on her. He showed up and showed out. He was everything a woman could ask for in a lover. No questions about it. She looked forward to knowing him better. In and out of the bedroom.

Turning over on her side, she noticed that his spot was empty. Figuring he went to the bathroom, she threw the covers back, getting out of bed, walking into the bathroom. He wasn't in plain sight. She pulled back the shower curtain thinking that he might be there. She didn't hear the water running, but she pulled back the shower curtain anyway just to make sure.

Maybe he's in the kitchen cooking me breakfast. That would be a nice surprise. I hope he can cook cause I'm hungry.

Skipping downstairs to the kitchen, she entered with a wide smile, but found disappointment again. He wasn't there either.

Fearing the worse, she rushed over to the window, pulling the curtain back, confirming what she suspected deep inside. His car wasn't there. Her heart sunk. It felt as if she couldn't breathe.

He left me. Why? What did I do wrong?

Her worst fear had come true. She was afraid that he'd sex her and leave. And he did.

He lied to me just to get my goodies. And I fell for it. I feel like the biggest fool. He had no damn intentions of getting to know me. Tears immediately came to her eyes. *I thought we shared something special. At least it felt that way.*

She quickly wiped away her tears, refusing to cry over a man that she barely knew. Yes, it hurt because she was so into him. He captured her heart without her even knowing it. Still, that didn't mean that he could play her. Determined to move on from this ordeal, she frantically wiped more tears away.

Put My Name On It

I'm nobody's punk. He might have gotten some pussy, but I refuse to let him get the best of me. I'm better than that. It'll take more than a fine rich man to break me.

She called her job and told them that she was coming in. They asked her if she could work over yesterday before she left work. She told them no at the time. She wanted her day off. Now that her plans fail through, she was ready to focus on anything but Marcel's disappearance. Working overtime would keep her mind off being stood up. She knew if she stayed at home, she would have a pity party for herself. That's the last thing she wanted to do.

"Fuck him," she screamed picking up an expensive family heirloom. The vase shattered against the front door as she slid down an adjacent wall in sorrow.

No matter how much she tried to hide her emotions, she couldn't. Before long, she was balled up on the floor crying her eyes out, wondering what went wrong.

I don't ever want to see his sorry ass again, she thought, wiping away fresh tears. *His ass is history!*

Chapter 9

Marcel walked into his office wondering where everyone was. It was empty which was weird. Knowing that he smelled like hot sweaty sex, he retreated to his deluxe office to freshen up. His office was equipped like a studio apartment, including a walk-in closet, shower, bath, and bed.

As he showered, he thought about Natalia. In the short time he'd known her, she captured a piece of him that no other woman ever has.

I'm going to call her as soon as I get dressed.

Promptly washing and then dressing, he raced to his office phone and dialed her number. His heart beat against his chest like a drum as he counted the rings. He had no idea what he was going to say when she answered. Relieved when the voicemail picked up, he cleared his throat prepared to leave a silky smooth message when his assistant walked in, interrupting his flow.

Put My Name On It

"I see you finally made it," Mia said, skipping into his office with a huge grin. "I called you at least ten times. Where you been?"

Marcel hung up. He decided to call Natalia back later. "What's good, Mia?" He wondered why she was acting like a kid high off candy.

"I got a surprise for you." Marcel eyed the giddy smile on her face as she clapped her hands with excitement.

The more she smiled, the more her joy seemed contagious. Marcel found himself smiling back. "Ok, tell me, what's up?"

Mia stood her ground. "I told you. It's a surprise. You'll have to wait and see."

Feeling the effects of her excitement, he began to anticipate the surprise. "So, when do I find out about this so called *surprise*?"

"In a little while. I'm going to take you to it."

Thoughts of calling Natalia quickly slipped Marcel's mind momentarily as he wondered what kind of surprise his assistant had for him. This wasn't the first time she surprised him. But it was the first time that he saw a twinkle in her eye.

Whatever it was had to be really big.

"Get your things and follow me," she exclaimed walking out of his office.

Marcel gathered his belongings and followed her outside. As they got into the limo waiting by the curb, he saw a woman across the street that had a flare about her that reminded him of Natalia. He wondered if she was awake by now.

He picked up his cell dialing Natalia's number again. Contacting her was all he could think of. Looking into Mia's cheerful face, he immediately ended the call, setting his phone down. He was so anxious to communicate with Natalia that he kept forgetting the fact that Mia was in earshot of his conversation.

Natalia would have to wait until after my surprise. When I can be alone and have privacy. Right now, I don't have that.

After being caught up in his thoughts of the previous night, he finally noticed that they were riding through O'Hare International Airport. "My surprise is here?"

"Yes," Mia exclaimed with the same enthusiasm.

Marcel wondered what kind of surprise would be at the airport. His eyes followed each terminal as they passed by. The suspense had his nerves shot. He was wrecking his brain trying to figure out what kind of surprise would be waiting for him at the airport. "Why can't you just tell me, Mia?"

"Relax," she said, leaning back, grinning. "You'll see soon enough."

Something about this didn't sit well with him. He had the strangest feeling he wasn't going to be as excited as she was when the surprise was finally revealed.

Put My Name On It

All kinds of things ran through his mind. He wondered if it was an ex-girlfriend, but quickly dismissed that idea. All those loose ends were completely tied up.

Then he wondered if it was his family giving him a surprise visit. It had been awhile since he'd seen them. He planned on making a trip back to New York, but work kept him so busy. *That has to be it. Mia is surprising me with my family.*

The limo driver pulled up in front of American Airlines. The driver got out and opened Marcel's door. "Your destination, sir."

Mia got out with an extra spring in her step. Marcel followed suit, looking around. He expected to see the familiar faces of his family. Instead all he saw was strangers. He knew something wasn't right when the driver walked around the limo, opening the trunk. His eyes zeroed in on the multiple suitcases.

What's the luggage for?

He turned to ask Mia what was going on, but she was nowhere in sight.

Her ass was standing right here. Where did she disappear to?

By the time he spotted her, she was walking inside the terminal, towards the ticket counter.

Ok, this has gone way too far. I need to know what the hell is going on. He marched through the double doors with a stern look on his face. "Tell me what's going on. NOW!" Marcel insisted. His outburst scared the older gentleman behind the ticket counter, waiting on Mia.

Mia took one look at Marcel's face and knew that she had better tell him what was going on. "Remember how you said that you wanted to do that big tour?"

"Yeah," Marcel said, still not fully understanding what she meant.

"And remember when you told me to make it happen by any means necessary?"

"What does that have to do with—" His voice trailed off when it finally sank in why they were at the airport.

"Well, I finally made it happen." Mia jumped up and down clapping her hands, giving him a gigantic hug. "It took me awhile to get everything in order, but I finally did it. An international tour!"

"WHAT!" Marcel said, louder than he anticipated, making the ticket agent tense again. "You mean to tell me we're leaving the United States and you're just now telling me?"

Mia stood there totally confused. "I thought this is what you wanted. You've been asking me to put this together for over a year. You said you didn't care how I did it, just get it done. I finally come through and you're mad? I don't get it."

Marcel sighed. She is absolutely correct. Yes, he had been asking her to book this tour for many months. That was before he met Natalia. Before he made plans with her today. Before he made a promise that he can't keep.

"No, you're right," he finally said, realizing that what he considered a dream is now coming true. Looking back at the terminal doors, he imagined the look on Natalia's face when she realized that he was going to stand her up.

Disappointment washed over him. He didn't know if he would ever be able to make things up to her. He just hoped that once the tour was over, she would allow him to come back into her life, and pick up where they left off.

"How much time do we have before we board?"

"Not much time," the ticket agent said. "It's almost time for takeoff."

With that being said, Marcel cursed under his breath and followed Mia into the security zone.

This tour couldn't have come at a worse time.

He wasn't sure how his time overseas was going to affect his personal life. But he was sure that he would find out once he returned.

Why do things have to be so damn complicated?

Chapter 10

After being gone for nearly nine months, Marcel was more than ready to come back to The States. The tour was a blast. He had the time of his life, but he was sick of eating foreign food, living out of suitcases, and hotel hopping.

No doubt, he was super home sick.

Not to mention, he lost his cell phone somewhere in between his ride to the airport and boarding the plane. Most of the numbers in his phone he managed to remember or Mia had as backup. All except for the one number he wanted most—Natalia's. He dialed every number combination he could think of before he finally gave up.

After playing phone tag with Cash a few times, he finally got in contact with him. Just as he suspected, Natalia didn't want nothing to do with him. And Karen wasn't about to give up her new number. From what Cash repeated, Marcel was on Natalia's shit list. She cursed the ground he walked on and never wanted to see him again.

Put My Name On It

Through the media, she heard about his international tour. Everywhere she turned there were promotions, concert tapings, contest giveaways, and die-hard fans recanting what an awesome event it was. For that reason, she didn't understand why Marcel never mentioned anything about a tour while he was bedding her.

Marcel knew that Natalia had a good right to be pissed off. He disappeared without an explanation. Although the events that took place were unexpected and out of his control, he knew that Natalia would never see things that way. She was hurt by his actions.

In most situations like this, Marcel would throw himself into his music, forgetting about everything and everyone. Not this time. Being on tour gave him a lot of time to think. Every night when he closed his eyes, he saw Natalia's beautiful face. His absence made him long to be in her presence even more. He needed to hear her sweet voice and lay next to her womanly curves.

If he could have turned back the hands of time, he would have tried harder to keep in contact. At least she would have known that he was still interested. And she would know what really happened—that he had no knowledge of the surprise tour until he was about to board the plane. He would have told her that while he was out of the country his feelings grew stronger. He'd confess that this unexpected time away just confirmed how he really felt about her since the moment they met.

No matter how much she despised him now, he planned on seeing her as soon as he got back to Chicago. He felt it was his duty to fix what he messed up.

The second he got in the limo, he gave the driver directions to Natalia's house. During the ride over, he wondered if he was making a mistake. *What if she hates me so much she won't even talk to me? I've been gone a long time. She might not even want me back. What if she moved on? Found someone else.*

Marcel exhaled. His thoughts were driving him crazy. He had so many things racing through his mind. The fact that he hadn't spoken to her in months left a bad taste in his mouth. Deep down inside, he knew he fucked up. Badly. Still, he couldn't help but try to get things back on track.

The driver double parked in front of Natalia's house. Marcel took another deep breath before coolly getting out, jogging up her walkway. He reached the front door and rang the bell. All kinds of things ran through his mind as he waited. *What will I say? How will I explain my disappearance? Does she still feel the same? Will things pick up where they left off?*

A tall blonde haired woman answered the door. "Yes, may I help you?"

Marcel stared at the stranger, wondering who the hell was she. Glancing upward at the address above his head, he thought maybe he had the wrong house. "Excuse me. I'm looking for Natalia. Is she here?"

The lady laughed as if he just told a joke. "Oh no, young man, I'm afraid not. This is my house now. She sold it to me."

Marcel's heart dropped to his stomach. "Sold?"

"Yes, she sold it about three months ago. Are you a friend of hers?"

"Um, yes, I am. I was out of the country for months. I had no idea. You wouldn't happen to have her contact information would you?"

"I don't have a phone number, but I do have an address. At least this was the address she gave me three months ago. I'll go get it for you." The lady left and came back with Natalia's address on a sticky note, handing it to him.

"Thank you," Marcel said, staring at it wondering why she sold her house. "Sorry to take up your time. I appreciate your help."

"No problem. Hope you find her."

"Thanks. Me too," Marcel mumbled as he walked away. *Natalia never mentioned that she was moving.*

Getting back into the limo, he told the driver to drop him off at home. In order to roll by Natalia's new address, he needed his own whip.

Arriving home, he looked around, making sure everything was in tack. Then, he took a hot shower and put on fresh clothes, making sure he was tight before hitting the streets again. Looking over at the mini bar, he really wanted to have a drink before riding out. Just a little something to take the edge off.

Nah, I can't have a drink. I need a clear head. Besides, I want to make a good impression.

After deciding against drinking, he walked outside and jumped into his ride. Rap blared from the radio. He turned it off popping in an old school R&B mix tape to easy his nerves. Looking at the sticky note one last time, he punched Natalia's new address into his navigation system. Once he adjusted the mirrors and seat, he pulled out of the parking garage on a mission to get his girl back.

Thirty minutes later, Marcel was driving down Natalia's block. He spotted her new house and began looking for a park. Just in case she was on one, he decided to park a few houses up.

Exiting the car, he rehearsed what he was going to say. A million thoughts crossed his mind. As he was about to cross the street, he saw Natalia walk out. He thought that seeing her after all this time would be a delight. He had no idea he would be seeing her with a gigantic stomach. His feelings of excitement instantly transformed to resentment.

This bitch is pregnant. I can't believe it. I've been waiting for her and she got knocked up by another nicca while I was gone. Ain't this some shit!

Put My Name On It

Usually, he would feel bad for calling a woman out of her name. Not this time. His feelings were crushed. He felt his words were justified. Natalia was fucking around with his heart.

Enraged, Marcel crossed the street with a pissy attitude, racing towards Natalia. She was about to catch it.

She moved on like I meant nothing to her. I feel like such a fool for wanting to pick up where we left off when she's pregnant by the next muthafucka.

He was so hurt that he wanted to cry. But being the man that he was, that wasn't going to happen. He refused to let her see him look weak.

"I guess you didn't think about waiting for me, huh?" Marcel said, walking up behind Natalia as she was about to open the trunk of her car.

She froze recognizing his voice right away. Her heart rate increased. She thought that she would never see him again. Taking a deep breath, she turned around facing him with her game face on. "What are you talking about?"

Not only was she shocked to see him, but she wondered how he found her. Nobody knew her new address but Karen. And she knew Karen wouldn't betray her like that.

"I guess I meant nothing to you, huh?" Marcel said, stepping closer to her, examining her huge belly. "I was just another man in your bed."

"Really? You trying me right now." She couldn't believe he had the nerve to blame this on her.

"I might be trying, but obviously, you did it," Marcel spat, referring to her tummy.

"YOU DISAPPEARED ON ME, REMEMBER?" she screamed. "I woke up and you were gone. You left me and you have the nerve to be pissed off. I don't think so, boo-boo. Try again."

"I didn't leave you," Marcel tried to explain. "I went on tour. There's a difference."

"And you couldn't tell me that beforehand? Before you seduced me into having sex with you." Marcel opened his mouth to explain, but Natalia put her hand in his face, shutting him up. "I don't want to hear your sorry ass lame excuses. What was I supposed to do? Put my life on hold for you? Wait around until you decided to pop your ass back up, nearly nine fucking months later? Get the hell outta my face, Marcel. You on some country-fried bullshit right now."

"I'm on bullshit? I wasn't gone that long and you already knocked up. You couldn't wait for me to get gone so you could open your legs for the next muthafucka." He stepped even closer practically pinning her against the trunk. "This my fuckin pussy!" he hollered. "I PUT MY NAME ON IT!"

Natalia looked at him like he had three heads. "What the hell you talking about? This my pussy. Attached to my damn body."

Put My Name On It

"Fuck that. I want answers." He was standing so close, he was pressing against her stomach.

"What! You owe me answers. I'm the one who woke up to an empty ass bed. I searched high and low for you." Natalia rolled her eyes, holding back tears. He had her so pissed off she wanted to knock him upside his head. "You promised to take me out the next day and I believed your lying ass. How stupid could I be? You played me like a groupie hoe."

Marcel got all in her face. As pissed off as he was, he couldn't deny the fact that he still had deep feelings for her. Being so close had his emotions going haywire. "I keep telling your hard of hearing ass, I didn't fuckin leave you."

"So what do you call it? You don't show your face until months later. What the hell is that? Cause it sounds like you dissed me."

Marcel fixed his mouth to say something back and Natalia shut him down again. "Fuck you, Marcel. There's nothing you can say to me. As of right now, you are a no good piece of shit. Another lying ass dog. Just come clean with me. You just wanted some pussy. Instead of being a real man and telling me that, you lied."

She blinked away tears. "Why the hell you come here? To make me feel even worse?" Natalia wiped away the few tears that fell. "Mission accomplished.

You got what you wanted. I feel like shit. Happy now? Leave me the hell alone."

Marcel wasn't happy at all. He still couldn't get pass the fact that she was pregnant. All he saw was images of another man up inside of her sugar walls. That drove him crazy. His eyes rested on her stomach.

"Did you think about how I would feel? Or was I just an afterthought? Or maybe you thought I'd come back and take care of you regardless. Use me because I got money, huh?" His mind drifted back to his ex and how she was playing him from the beginning.

Natalia noticed him staring at her baby bump. "Don't worry about my baby. He's none of your concern. I'm gonna make sure my son is well taken care of. We don't need nobody to help us, especially not your sorry ass. I have everything in place. You and your money can go to hell."

"Whatever." Marcel felt his heart breaking as he tried to hide his pain. "Do you know that all I thought about on tour was you? And this is what you do to me? You just like all the other woman. Good for nothing, easy, and full of drama."

"I'm done talking to you." Her stomach began to hurt from arguing with him, but she refused to show him that he was getting the best of her. "Just leave. I have nothing else to say to you." She waved him off, hoping he would just go. When he didn't move she yelled, "STEP THE HELL OFF!"

Put My Name On It

As stubborn as he was he had to have the last word. Marcel was hurting so bad that he wanted to slap her face, but he didn't hit women, and he wasn't about to start. She was pregnant and he respected that regardless of how thing went down between them. "Fuck you!"

He gave her an evil stare before he stepped back, walking away. He knew that if he kept talking to her, he was going to go against everything that he believed in, possibly putting his hands on her. Ringing her neck sounded like a good idea at the moment.

Natalia felt a sharp sting in her side that nearly knocked her to her knees. It was so intense that she held onto the trunk of her car, doubled over in pain.

"She ain't shit," Marcel repeated over and over as he walked across the street to his car with tears in his eyes. Confronting Natalia didn't give him the closure he thought it would. It left him with a headache, a queasy stomach, and suppressing his true feelings.

Near his car, he had the sudden urge to throw up, but nothing came up. He doubled over gagging a few times. *What the hell is wrong with me?* It felt like someone had punching him in his balls. The pain was unbearable. Breathing rapidly, he held onto his car trying to catch his breath. Sweat gathered on his forehead as his mind tried to figure out what the fuck just happened. Standing there for a few moments with his eyes closed, he took deep breaths, trying to block out the discomfort.

Chapter 11

Rage filled Marcel as soon as the pain subsided. He jumped into his car about to pull off. *Damn, I can't believe after everything she did to me, I'm still thinking about her ass. What the fuck is wrong with me?* He hit the steering wheel so hard the whole car shook. *I need to man the fuck up.*

It took everything in him not to go completely off. The way he felt he could have blacked out and beat her ass like a pimp does his hoe. Taking one last look at Natalia before he left, he noticed her bent over on the trunk of her car. She was hardly able to stand and looked to be in a lot pain.

Putting the car in drive, ready to pull off, he wanted to say *fuck her*, but he couldn't. His heart wouldn't allow him to. Seeing her in pain didn't sit well with him. He threw the car in reverse, backing down the street until his car was parallel to hers.

"You alright?" he asked, rolling down the passenger's side window.

Natalia winced in pain. "Yeah. I'm fine. I think I just upset the baby."

Drive away. This ain't your problem. Marcel sighed. He wanted to stay in his feelings and drive away, but he got out the car instead. Natalia yelled out in pain when he tried to help her stand straight. Her face was flushed and beads of sweat covered her forehead. "Are you sure you're ok?"

Natalia dropped her tough girl exterior, holding her stomach in extreme pain. "I don't know for sure, but I think I'm going into labor."

At that moment, Marcel totally forgot about his anger towards her. He just wanted to get her to the hospital. No matter how he felt, he didn't want her or the baby to lose their lives because of his selfishness.

"I'm getting you to the hospital," he said, putting one arm around her waist, helping her stand. "Can you walk?"

"Aaaaaah," she yelled breathing rapidly after taking a few steps forward. She looked completely disheveled. Her neat ponytail was now a loose knot hanging on her shoulders. Her clothes were sweaty. Her face was pale.

Before helping her into his car, Marcel got a blanket out the trunk and placed it on the passenger's seat before she sat down. He didn't want his new car ruined. He closed her door and raced around to the driver's side. "Do you have a hospital of preference?"

Put My Name On It

"My doctor is affiliated with all the hospitals in this area." Natalia clinched her stomach in pain. "OOOOOOOOOOH!"

"What's wrong?" All this was new to him. He didn't know what else to do, but get her to the hospital as soon as possible. Her screams had his nerves on overdrive.

"My water just broke," Natalia said, looking at the messy puddle on the floor of his car.

"Shit!" Marcel yelled. "I just got this car. You couldn't wait?"

Natalia gave him a nasty look. "Does it look like I can wait? Just hurry up and get me there. The baby's coming." Marcel was about to pull off when Natalia stopped him, tapping his arm. "I need my labor bag. It's inside the house by the front door."

"What you need that for?"

She winced in pain. "You don't know nothing, do you?"

Marcel snapped at her. "How the hell would I know? I never had a baby before. All this shit is new to me."

Natalia held out her house key, almost scratching his face. "Just get my bag, please." She rolled her eyes. "It has everything I need for the hospital. And don't forget to call Karen."

Marcel snatched the key from her and got out the car with an attitude. He didn't understand the importance of this labor bag. It wasn't like the hospital didn't have everything she needed. He quickly grabbed the labor bag and called Karen, getting her voicemail. He left a brief message for her and Cash and raced into city traffic heading full speed to the hospital.

Normally, Natalia would have made him slow down, but she was so preoccupied with labor pains that she couldn't even think straight. The faster he drove, the faster she would be out of pain. Parking out front, Marcel rushed through the emergency room doors, approaching the first nurse he saw.

"Excuse me, Miss," he said politely, tugging on the nurse's sleeve. "My girlfriend, I mean—" He was about to correct himself when the nurse gave him an impatient look. Thinking more of Natalia and the baby he continued. "She's in labor."

The frown on the nurse's face changed to concern. "Where's she at?"

Marcel raced out of the emergency doors taking the nurse right to Natalia. The nurse quickly assessed the situation realizing that Natalia was in no condition to walk. She darted back inside to get a wheelchair.

"How far are your contractions, honey?" the nurse asked Natalia.

Marcel chimed in answering for her. "About every six minutes." Natalia and the nurse stared at Marcel. "What?" he questioned. "That's how often she cries out in pain."

Put My Name On It

The nurse helped Natalia into the wheelchair and pushed her straight to labor and delivery. Marcel walked swiftly behind them, wondering if Natalia would be ok. He didn't want to admit it, but seeing her in so much pain had him troubled. He was so worried about her that he started to feel sympathy pains.

Labor and delivery was chaotic.

Marcel was right by her side when her doctor and two nurses rushed into the room. All of a sudden he felt ambushed even though they were all polite introducing themselves. One of the nurses helped Natalia remove her clothes so she could put on the hospital gown. Meanwhile the other nurse rushed around the room, prepping it.

Marcel got a good look at Natalia's stomach as she undressed. She was huge. He felt bad for going off on her. Deep down inside, he knew that if he didn't make her so upset she wouldn't have gone into premature labor.

"Are you staying?" the nurse asked Marcel while starting an IV.

He was so enthralled with the antics of Natalia being in labor that he didn't know if he was even allowed to stay. He was about to ask her if he should stay, but she looked to be in so much pain. "Yes, I'm staying."

He felt that was the least he could do after leaving her so unexpectedly. He owed her that much. Aiming to be as supportive as possible, he slipped his hand into hers while the doctor checked her cervix.

"Can I get something for the pain, Dr. Meska," Natalia mumbled in agony.

"Of course," he responded. "The nurse will take care of that. It won't be too long and the baby will be here." He stood, taking off his gloves. "Are you ready for the baby to come?"

Natalia gave a sluggish smile. "Yes. I don't think anyone is more ready to be a mother than me. I'm going to love him with everything I have."

When she said that, Marcel gained a newfound respect for her. No matter what was going on, Natalia was ready to welcome her baby into this world and love him unconditionally. Although, this wasn't planned, he was happy to be a part of the whole experience. It was something about the birth of a baby that made him just a little sensitive.

Chapter 12

Natalia was fully dilated and ready to bring her first born child into this world.

Marcel knew she didn't want him there, but he ignored her nasty looks, holding her hand regardless.

The doctor told her to push. She squeezed Marcel's hand with all her might. It felt like she broke all four of his fingers. He wanted to scream out in pain, but the scream got stuck in the back of his throat. All he could do was breath heavy as if he was in labor too.

Several pushes into it, Natalia was exhausted, falling onto her back in tears. "I can't believe he's not out yet. I can't push no more. I'm so tired."

Marcel dabbed her face with a wet cloth like the nurse told him to. The more he dabbed, the more he pissed Natalia off. She took the cloth out of his hand, slinging it across the room. It hit the wall hard before tumbling to the floor. "Don't touch me!"

Marcel wanted to ask her if she was crazy, but he knew better than to go toe to toe with a woman in labor. The crazed look on Natalia's face expressed that she might kill him if he opened his mouth. Biting his tongue, he gritted his teeth, keeping quiet.

Natalia gained a little strength, sitting upright. She gave a strong push like Dr. Meska told her before falling back on the bed, fatigued.

"Waaaaaaaa," cried the golden-colored baby with dark brown hair and light brown eyes.

"It's a boy," Dr. Meska said with pride, placing the baby boy on Natalia's chest.

Marcel smiled at the newborn. He was so little and cute. He wanted to hold him too.

"Do you want to cut the umbilical cord?" the nurse asked.

Marcel didn't know what she was talking about but he agreed anyway. "Sure."

She placed the scissors in his hand guiding him through the process.

Feeling more attached to the baby, Marcel held his little hand while he was in Natalia's arms. She was still trying to catch her breath from the intensity of being in labor.

Just when her breathing seemed to be returning to normal, another sharp pain hit her like a ton of bricks. "OWWW! OWW! OWWWW!" she hollered at the top of her lungs.

Dr. Meska buried his head between her legs. "It's probably the placenta," he said, baffled. "However, it shouldn't hurt like this." He leaned in closer to get a better look.

"What's the matter, Doc?" Marcel asked noticing the bewildered look on the doctor's face. "Is she going to be alright?"

Ignoring Marcel, Dr. Meska focused on Natalia. "I need you to push again."

Natalia lifted her head in awe. "What! I thought this was all over. Why am I pushing again?"

The doctor repeated sternly. "I need you to push again, Natalia."

Marcel took the baby out of her arms so that she could do what the doctor said.

Just as Natalia was about to protest, she felt another contraction hit her with full force. Aaaaaaaaaah!" she yelled pushing involuntarily.

"Waaaaaaa! Waaaaaa! Waaaaaa!"

Natalia couldn't believe that she was hearing the cries of another baby. *What the hell*?

Before she could ask what's happening, Dr. Meska held up another baby. "Congratulations! This one is a girl."

Natalia stared at the baby in a state of shock. "Oh No! You got to be kidding me. Not another baby. Doctor, you never said anything about twins." She rolled her eyes and shook her head eyeballing the surprise baby girl who had a golden complexion and curly hair like her brother. Her eyes were green.

"I can't believe we have twins."

"We?" Marcel said in shock.

"Yes. And this is all your damn fault. I didn't even want to have sex that night."

Thinking about it carefully, the time of conception and the length of time he was gone all adds up. When he did the math, he was gone nearly nine months and she was almost nine months pregnant.

"Are you ready to cut the umbilical cord again?" the nurse asked, breaking his concentration.

"Sure," Marcel replied in a slight daze. He placed the baby boy back in Natalia's arms and cut the baby girl's umbilical cord. He thought he was in awe when he saw the little boy, but when he held the baby girl he fell madly in love with her. Despite her light eyes, Marcel knew she was his. After taking a closer look at the baby boy, he realized he was a splitting image of him when he was a child.

Exhausted, Natalia leaned back, feeling like she was about to pass out. Her body felt like she'd been in a car accident. Everything hurt. Glancing up at Marcel, she caught him eyeing the kids with a strange look on his face.

I know he's not questioning if these babies are his. I will cut him if he denies my kids.

"She's yours, if that's what you're thinking," Natalia snapped. "Green eyes run in my family." She exhaled loudly expressing her instant disgust. "Don't deny my baby."

Marcel picked up on her attitude and quickly tried to defuse the situation. "Look, I can't change what happened in the past. I had a tour planned before I met you. I came home as soon as the tour ended. You see, I'm here. I came looking for you."

Natalia blinked back tears. "It doesn't matter. You missed my whole pregnancy. I went through it all by myself."

"But I'm here now. I want to be here for you and the kids. If I knew you were pregnant, I would have cancelled the tour, but I didn't know. You never told me."

"I tried to call you. I dialed your number over and over. All I got was voicemail."

Marcel wanted to kick himself for losing his phone. "I lost my phone," he said in defeat. "It sounds like a lame answer, but it's true. I promise."

"Your promises mean nothing to me." She sighed loudly again. "I wouldn't have gotten pregnant if it wasn't for you. I slept with you because you wanted me to. Then you made empty promises that you couldn't keep, leaving me to deal with the consequences of our loving making. ALL ALONE!"

"Natalia, it wasn't like that," Marcel said, feeling horrible for happened. "I can't change the past—"

"Yeah. Yeah. Yeah. I heard it before...but you can change the future," Natalia said finishing his sentence with an attitude. "Save it for the next chick you get pregnant."

"You act like I did it on purpose."

Beep. Beep. Beep. Beep.

The machine next to Natalia's bed was going erratic. All of a sudden, Natalia began gasping for air. One of the nurses rushed to her aid. The other nurse took the baby boy out of her arms, rushing him to the nursery.

"What happened? What's going on?" Marcel asked holding his daughter close to his chest. The loud sound from the machine had him really worried. He didn't want to admit it, but he was actually scared that he might lose Natalia. "Why is that machine going crazy? Is she ok?"

The nurse continued to help Natalia, ignoring Marcel's frantic questions.

"Why won't you answer me?" Marcel asked, slightly raising his voice.

The nurse who took the baby boy to the nursery came back and gently removed the baby girl from Marcel's grasp, placing her in the nursery beside her twin brother.

"Can someone please tell me what's going on?" Marcel looked on as Natalia continued to be in distress.

Put My Name On It

"Look, if you care anything about the mother of your children, I suggest you leave now!" the nurse assisting Natalia demanded.

Marcel stood in disbelief as Natalia's heart rate increased right along with her blood pressure. He wasn't about to take a step anywhere. Like clockwork, the nurse who took his children returned just in time to usher him out.

"I'm not trying to get into your business, young man, but you can't stay," the nurse told him as they stood in the hallway. Marcel was about to speak up and she stopped him. "Listen, I can't imagine how you feel. And I don't know the full story between you two, but what I do know is you love her and those kids. And for that reason, I need you to allow us to do our job and help your kid's mother. That means you have to leave."

Marcel nodded in agreement, but it still didn't change how he felt.

"Why don't you go home and get some rest," the nurse suggested. "You can visit tomorrow. She should be much better by then."

Marcel read between the lines. His conversation stressed Natalia out. That's why she was in distress. Thinking back on it all, he figured that it would be best if he left too. "I guess you're right. I don't want to cause her any more pain. She needs to be here for our kids."

85

"Exactly. Just give her some space. I'm sure she'll come around. Sometimes it takes a moment for a woman scorned."

Marcel didn't question what the nurse said. He was sure she overheard their conversation and put the pieces together. Besides, giving Natalia some space might help after all. He was sure that if he didn't play by her rules, he would lose his family.

Doing as the nurse asked of him, Marcel reluctantly left Natalia and the twins behind.

Chapter 13

Marcel walked towards the hospital entrance with his head hung low. His emotions were at an all-time high. The day's events replayed over and over in his mind taking a toll on him. As happy as he was to be a father, he was equally as sad knowing that Natalia viewed him as a deadbeat. That really stung.

"I was shocked that you were back in town and didn't come check me out," Cash said, stepping into Marcel's path, snapping him out of his thoughts. Marcel didn't see Karen or Cash as they were coming into the hospital. In his state of confusion, he forgot all about calling them.

"Oh, what's up?" Marcel said, trying to play things off. He stepped closer giving his boy dap and a one-arm hug. He couldn't believe that he was so deep in thought that he about to walk right pass his best friend. "I see you got my message."

Cash eyed his boy immediately wondering what was wrong. "Yeah, I came as soon as I could."

"Congratulations," Karen said, hugging Marcel. She could tell that he had a lot on his mind by the spaced out look on his face. Knowing Natalia, she figured her girl probably ripped him a new asshole for going M.I.A. while she was pregnant.

Likewise, Cash knew his boy wasn't himself. "You must be in shock after finding out she was pregnant. Cause I was in shock when I got your message."

Marcel was so disgusted with everything that just happened. He couldn't even look Cash in the eye. "Shocked ain't even the word, yo" he exclaimed, staring at the carpet.

Karen knew that Cash and Marcel needed a moment alone so she excused herself. "Cash, why don't you meet me upstairs? I'm going to check on Natalia." She leaned in hugging Marcel again, kissing him on the cheek. "Everything will work itself out. I'm sure of it," she whispered in his ear before walking away.

As soon as Karen left, Cash began apologizing. "Man, I swear to you, I didn't know shit. You know I would have told you about something this serious. That's my word."

"Yeah, man, I know," Marcel said, finally looking Cash in the eye.

"Karen didn't tell me a damn thing. I been asking her to stay out of y'all drama and she put her face all up in it."

Marcel shrugged it off. "Don't be mad at her. She was just sticking up for her girl. That's what she supposed to do. The same way we hold each other down."

"Yeah, I guess so," Cash said with a scowl on his face. He still felt Karen was wrong. "So, what did Natalia have? A boy or a girl?"

"Both," Marcel replied with an attitude.

Cash nearly swallowed the mint he just popped into his mouth. "Come again?"

"You heard me, man" Marcel said, cracking a smile for the first time.

"Are you saying she had twins?"

Marcel nodded.

"Damn! What the fuck did you do to her that night? You took beating the pussy up to the next level. Didn't you?"

"You wild." All Marcel could do is laugh as he thought about how crazy the sex was that night. "I told you I was going to put my name on it."

"Naw, you wild." Cash continued laughing as he ran down the facts. "Here's how I see it. You took her out, fucked her the same night, and got her pregnant with not one baby but two. What kind of super sperm you holding?"

Marcel laughed harder after hearing Cash's viewpoint. This is one reason why they've been boys so long. Cash was hilarious.

"You got a point." Marcel stopped laughing, stressing over his situation again. "But now she don't want nothing to do with me. I fucked up bad, bro. And now my kids are going to be fucked up too." Marcel was getting worked up all over again. "I don't want my kids to grow up without a father like I did."

Cash knew his boy was feeling Natalia from all of their conversations. He never interacted with a woman like he did with her. Nor did he talk about a woman like he talked about her.

"Hold up, you not out the game yet, homie. She got two babies to take care of. She don't have a choice but to come around and see things your way."

"Yo, you weren't up there. She hates my fuckin guts. You should have seen how she looked at me, like she wished I would drop dead. I believe if she wasn't in so much pain, she would have spit on me."

"Naw, Natalia don't hate you, dawg. She loves your dirty draws. Believe that. Why you think she acting out? Cause she's hurt. Give her some space and play by her rules for a little while. Then drop game on her."

"I don't know," Marcel said feeling totally defeated. He wasn't sure if he was up for the challenge.

"Hell, if all fails give her the same dick you gave her months ago. I'm certain she'll come back then." Cash grinned from ear to ear thinking about how well that always worked on Karen.

Put My Name On It

"This shit is too complicated," Marcel said, feeling a headache coming on full throttle.

"See, that's your problem. You thinking like a man."

Marcel chuckled. "Cause I am a man. How the hell am I supposed to think?"

Cash stared at his friend, looking him dead in the eye so he knew he was serious. "No, you don't get it. In order to be in a relationship with a woman, you have to think like one. Get in touch with your feelings and shit. How do you think I figured Karen out? I thought about what I would do and then did the opposite. I'm telling you, the shit works like a charm."

Cash had Marcel's full attention now. "You think that's really going to work?"

"Damn right it will. You gotta see things from her point of view. Connect with her emotionally. Find out why she feels the way she do. Once you figure that out, you can correct any situation with a woman."

Marcel heard Cash loud and clear. What he was saying felt like part two of what the nurse upstairs just told him. The more he thought about it, the more it was all starting to make perfect sense.

"Feel what I'm saying?" Cash asked Marcel, noticing the new gleam of hope.

Marcel nodded. "Yeah, I think I get it."

Cash patted his boy on the back. "Go home and get your game tight. And get plenty of rest cause you gonna need it. You got two crying ass babies to deal with."

"I know right," Marcel said rubbing his temples, trying to stop the headache that was inevitable.

"Glad I'm not your ass." Cash smiled. "I still can't believe you knocked her up with twins after fucking one night."

Marcel shook his head in disbelief. "Yeah, me either."

Chapter 14

Everything that Cash and the nurse said definitely put things in perspective. Once Marcel put himself in Natalia's shoes he realized that it was his responsibility to win her back. She had every right to be pissed off at him. It was all his fault and he intended on dealing with her nasty attitude until she changed her mind. Exhausted and mentally drained, he retreated to bed, falling into a deep sleep right away.

The next day, Marcel woke up fully rested. Feeling more in control, he strutted through the hospital ready for today's visit. He had his game face on. Ready to go toe to toe with Natalia. His main focus was sensitivity and understanding, knowing that's what she needed right now.

Marcel took a deep breath and swallowed his pride before he approached Natalia's hospital room. The door was closed so he politely knocked waiting for her to say he could enter.

"Come in," she replied in a tired voice.

Princess Diamond

When he entered, Natalia was breastfeeding their son. Their eyes locked briefly before Natalia quickly looked away. Marcel walked in closing the door and proceeded over to her carrying the vase with a beautiful rose bouquet. He brought her a mixture of white and pink roses with a pink bow tied around them. He also had teddy bears for the kids.

"These are for you," he said, sitting the vase down by her bedside.

Natalia's eyes scanned the flowers. *Those flowers are nice, but I'm not going to tell him that. He's gotta do more than some damn flowers to get in good with me.*

"Thank you," she said dryly, suppressing the urge to roll her eyes and suck her teeth.

"Is there anything you need for the kids?" Marcel asked sincerely. It was his attempt to make conversation and get back in her good graces.

"Not sure." Natalia didn't even look his way. "I'll let you know."

"Ok," Marcel said, leaning on the bedrail. *This is going to be harder than I thought.*

He watched her breastfeed his son. Her breast were so full, so swollen. Watching his son suck on a breast that once belonged to him made him feel some kinda way. Staring at the baby, he suppressed the urge to take him back to the nursery so that he could take his place.

Put My Name On It

Marcel chuckled realizing that he was envious of a newborn.

"What's so funny?" Natalia asked eyeing him suspiciously.

"Nothing." A smile formed on Marcel's face as he continued to fanaticize about sucking on Natalia's thick nipple. It turned him on to say the least, making his dick throb in his jeans. *I can't just stand here and watch my son get all the action.*

Marcel leaned forward about to pick up his son and mess up his whole plan when the nurse came in holding the baby girl.

Natalia looked at him crazy.

Before they could exchange words, the nurse handed Marcel his daughter. The moment he held his baby girl, all sexual thoughts about Natalia immediately disappeared and a pout came across his face. However, his mood changed once the baby settled in the crook of his arm.

The nurse noticed his change in demeanor, but refused to speak on it. "Here are the paternity papers to sign," she said, handing them to Marcel. "And if you want a DNA test we can do that too. Just let me know when I return."

The nurse left Marcel holding his daughter, staring at the paternity papers. He sighed loudly, making Natalia's eyes shift from their son to him.

95

I don't feel like looking at this right now. I want to fix things with Natalia. As he complained silently, his eyes zeroed in on the names of his children. *Marcelius and Marcelina. She named the kids after me? After everything I've done? I definitely have to make this right now.*

Natalia fixed her eyes on Marcel, watching him closely. She picked up on the indecisive expression on his face as he stared at the paternity papers. "Don't tell me you're still having doubts." she said, fighting back tears. "I can't believe you carrying me like this."

Shame consumed her. Just the possibility of Marcel wanting a paternity test made her regret having sex with him, once again. "These babies look just like you, but if you want a paternity test, go for it. It's your damn money. Do you, boo!"

Marcel was so caught up in the fact that she named the kids after him that he didn't hear a word she said. "You named them after me? Why?"

Natalia blinked rapidly fighting off tears. "Why not, Marcel? They're yours."

Marcel finally looked over at Natalia, realizing how emotional she was. He had no idea why she was so distraught, but he assumed it had something to do with the paternity papers. She was probably tripping because he hadn't signed them yet.

"I never said they weren't mine." Marcel eyeballed both of his babies. He knew they were his. "I was just amazed that you named them after me. Their names are beautiful."

"Whatever," Natalia said, wiping away the few tears that fell. "You are so tired right now."

"Let me make this right." Marcel placed Marcelina in the bed next to her so he could read the paternity papers. After reading them over, he signed them, and handed them to Natalia to sign. "Are we good?"

"Don't act like you doing me a favor." Natalia was ready to slap the piss out of him. "You thought I was pregnant by someone else, remember?"

Marcel sighed. He couldn't even get mad because he jumped to conclusions instead of asking her. "You're right. I'm sorry for that. I shouldn't have said it, but I've signed the papers. I acknowledge that both children are mine. I want to be there for them. Not just financially either."

"I don't have a problem with that, Marcel."

They locked eyes again. This time neither one of them broke the stare. The chemistry was still there. There was no denying that they both felt a strong connection.

Marcel thought she was absolutely beautiful. From her glowing skin to her long flowing hair. It grew a lot over the months, framing her face perfectly. He didn't want to admit it, but he was still madly in love with her.

Marcelina's cries made Marcel break their staring match. He picked her up, cradling her in his arms. Holding her close and rocking her gently, he talked sweetly to his little princess. "Shhhh. Daddy's right here." He kissed her nose. "I got you, little lady. You're safe with me."

Natalia observed Marcel's interaction with their daughter. As much as she loved her babies, she still wondered if having sex with Marcel was a big mistake.

Would he still want me if I didn't give birth to his kids? I'm not so sure. Seems like he only stepped up after the babies were born. Sounds like he is just telling me what I want to hear to win me over. Only time will tell. Cause if he is lying no telling what I might do to his ass.

"Time to switch," Natalia said, removing her breast from Marcelius' mouth. "I need to feed her."

Marcel laid Marcelina in her lap and picked up his son. "Hey, little man." He planted a kiss on his chubby cheeks. "Do you know who I am? I'm your daddy. I can't wait until you get older so we can watch basketball together. Can you say New York Knicks?" Marcelius smiled at his father as if he understood everything he just said. "That's right. We're Giants fans too." Marcelius cooed at his father's response.

Natalia found herself smiling as she listened.

Holding Marcelius made him proud. He was a mini version of him. He never thought about being a father, but now that his kids were here, he couldn't imagine life without them.

"You and your sister are two of the best things that ever happened to me." He kissed the baby's tiny hand. "Well, besides my career and your Mommy. Without her you wouldn't be here."

Natalia didn't comment, but hearing Marcel admit how he felt made her less angry at him.

"Isn't this a sight? A baby for the each of you," the nurse said walking over to Marcel, all smiles. "Did you sign—"

"Here you go," Marcel said, nearly smacking the nurse in the face with the paternity papers. That wasn't his intention, however, he didn't want her stirring up any unnecessary drama. "Can we get a copy, please?"

"Sure," she stated before leaving the room again.

Marcel caught the sour look on Natalia's face. He had no idea what that was all about. "Let me take you and the babies home from the hospital?"

"I've already made arrangements." Natalia closed her eyes, refusing to look at him. She felt tears stinging her eyelids again. It was all too much. She never expected to see him again. In her mind, he was gone forever. She had it all planned out, being a single mother. Out of nowhere he shows up, throwing a monkey wrench in her plans.

"Please," he begged. "It would mean a lot to me."

Be strong, girl. This man doesn't have a hold on your heart unless you let him. Stick to your plan.

"I don't think that's a good idea. We're not together and I don't want you to think that because we have kids that you owe me something. Besides, I made all these plans when I couldn't get in contact with you. It is what it is, Marcel."

In response, he thought about snapping off and saying something slick, putting her in her place. Kissing her ass was a little too hard. "So how do you want to do this? I'm just asking because I plan on seeing my kids."

Natalia finally looked at him, rolling her eyes as tears fell. "I don't know, but don't worry. I will make sure that you are a part of their lives. I wouldn't keep you from them. I'm not that cruel."

Marcel was about to address her last statement, but decided to let it go instead. "And what about us?" he inquired, hoping for the best.

Natalia shrugged her shoulders. "What about it?" She wanted nothing more in the world than to be with him. She just didn't see how that was going to happen.

Marcel felt his temper rising. There was only so much holding back he could do. Eventually, he was going to let loose. What pissed him off even more was the fact that he knew he deserved all the shade Natalia was giving him. Still, his pride wouldn't allow him to handle her tongue lashing. Her words hurt more that she knew.

Digging deep inside, he found the strength to commit to his original plan, which was more of a challenge then what he thought. He needed to leave before he said something stupid. Cutting his visit short was the only way to prevent that.

Marcel kissed his sleeping son before laying him down. "I'm about to leave," he announced walking over to the other side of the bed, kissing Marcelina. He wanted to kiss Natalia too, but blew her a kiss instead.

"But you just got here." Natalia tried to hide her disappointment but it showed all over her face. Torn between her heart and her head, she felt alone and very afraid. "Can't you stay a little longer?" As much grief as she gave him deep down inside she felt that if he left he'd be walking out on her again.

Marcel stood near the side of the bed, holding Marcelina's tiny hand. Natalia's sad expression let him know that she still cared, which gave him the glimpse of hope. That's what he needed to fight for their relationship. "Well, maybe I can stay a little longer. Under one condition though."

"What's that?" Natalia said, locking eyes with him once again.

"You let me bring you and the babies home from the hospital."

Natalia wanted to say no. This time she couldn't reject his request. Something wouldn't let her. "Alright. Just make sure you have two car seats because we can't leave the hospital without them."

Marcel grinned from ear to ear. "I'll get whatever you need as long as I can bring you home."

He stopped playing with the baby and leaned in, giving Natalia a soft kiss. She welcomed the kiss as if she initiated it. Marcel caressed Natalia's face, enjoying it to the fullest. She enjoyed it too, grabbing the back of his head, pulling him even closer. The kiss had Marcel turned on. He wanted to climb in the bed with her.

They kissed hungrily forgetting all about Marcelina who was wedged between them. If it wasn't for her loud screams, they might not have stopped.

"Wow!" Marcel backed up with his eyes still on Natalia. Her eyes were on him too. He studied her as she bit her bottom lip. The passion they just shared was indescribable. That kiss sealed the deal. He had no doubt that she still belonged to him.

Feeling the same way, Natalia couldn't help but to have a cheesy grin as she tended to the baby. She knew that if Marcelina didn't start crying, they'd still be kissing. Despite the fact of just giving birth, her kitty was hot for him.

I won't make it six weeks if he kisses me like that again.

Put My Name On It

"Thank you for changing your mind." Marcel said honestly. "I'm going to do right. I promise."

"You're welcome," Natalia said, knowing she made the right decision.

Chapter 15

Natalia made no excuses about losing the fifty pounds that she gained during pregnancy. She had to get back in shape after having the twins. Fitting into her pre-pregnancy wardrobe was a priority. Diet and exercise was her only mission for six weeks. She was determined to go to her checkup weighing exactly what she did before conception. It was going to be hard work but she was determined to make it happen.

And she kept her promise to Marcel allowing him to keep the babies whenever he wanted. The twins spent so much time with him at his condo that he had a nursery set up. When he wasn't cooing over the babies, he was buying them all kind of gifts. Being a father was more fulfilling then what he expected. On more than one occasion, he stated that he never felt as alive as he did in the presence of his kids. He loved them more than his music, which he didn't even think was possible.

There was only thing missing in his life was— Natalia. Secretly, Marcel longed to be with her making their family whole. They were getting along great co-parenting but that's not what he wanted. He wanted her to be his woman. It was hard falling back and waiting for the right time to execute his plan. Especially when he was constantly around her.

By the fifth week, he couldn't wait any longer. He was either going to go crazy or make his move. Waltzing into Natalia's house with a baby carrier in each hand, he was ready to take things to the next level.

"Good Afternoon." Marcel kissed Natalia on the cheek.

"Good Afternoon," she replied turning on her heels, walking into the kitchen.

Marcel sat the sleeping babies down in the living room and followed Natalia into the kitchen. *Damn, her ass is still fat. I gotta have her. Tonight.*

"Thanks for keeping up with the kids. This weight loss regime has been brutal. But I don't care. I refuse to look fat and sloppy. "

Marcel's eyes wandered over her body, admiring her curvy shape. "You look good to me."

"That's because I've been working at it for five weeks straight. Exercising like a manic and starving like a model. And I've lost a lot, but I still have a little more to lose."

"Starving maniac, huh?" Marcel repeated. "That sounds real crucial."

"That's what I feel like."

They both laughed at Natalia's analogy.

"How about you let me do something nice for you? For all your hard work."

"No," Natalia fired off quickly. She felt there was an ulterior motive behind his gesture.

"C'mon, just a way to celebrate your accomplishments. You deserve to be pampered. Let me do that much for you," Marcel said, trying to win her over with his charm.

Natalia stood there, wondering what his angle was. His words said that he wanted to do something special for her, but the cute smirk on his face said otherwise. *Look at him standing there looking like a handsome devil.* "And just how do you plan on celebrating?"

Marcel grinned, knowing that he was about to get his way. "Spa treatment and dinner. That's all."

Natalia looked at him sideways. "That's it. Nothing more?"

"Like what?" he asked, playing dumb. He knew what she was referring to—sex. No way was he about to admit that he planned on ending the celebration with a night of hot, freaky sex.

Natalia eyed him suspiciously. "And who's keeping the babies?"

"I already talked to your grandmother. Everything's in order. All you have to do is say yes." Marcel leaned across the counter staring at her with anticipation. He knew his intense stare was breaking her down by the way she kept on fidgeting.

Natalia studied him a little while longer before she finally agreed. "Ok, I guess you're right. I do need a break. I've been pushing myself really hard. It would be nice to relax a little and have some fun."

"Exactly." Marcel stood to his feet with a sly grin. He had been patient for what seemed like forever trying to be the perfect father and a good man to her as well. "The limo will be here to pick you up in an hour. After the spa treatment, you'll be dropped off at the restaurant. I'll be there waiting on you."

Marcel handed Natalia the spa certificate. Her mouth opened wide when she saw everything her package contained. He hooked her up with an amazing New Mommy Package. It consisted of four indulging hours of a full body massage, facial and skin treatments, waxing, hair care, manicure, and pedicure.

Unable to contain her joy, she squealed in excitement throwing her arms around Marcel's neck, squeezing him tight. Marcel held her small waist, elated to be so close again, taking a whiff of her sweet scent. He wanted to pick her up and place her on the counter, burying his face between her legs.

Relax, he said to himself, trying to control the urge. He pulled away from her just in time. One second more and she would have felt his erection poking through.

Princess Diamond

While Marcel's mind was on sex, Natalia's mind was on the tranquility of a spa day. She couldn't wait to be pampered. "I better get ready since I only have an hour."

"Enjoy." Marcel said, exiting the kitchen, grabbing the twins. He was super happy that his plan worked like a magic. "I'll see you in a few."

"Ok," Natalia said, giving him a dainty wave as she headed upstairs.

Chapter 16

The limo pulled up in front of Sigel's Restaurant. Natalia stepped out striking a pose in red stilettos with a form-fitted red wrap dress that showed off her toned body. She looked absolutely amazing. Nobody would ever guess that she gave birth to twins weeks ago.

The spa did wonders for her spirit. Not only did she look good, but she felt good too. Being pampered was just the thing she needed to get her confidence back. After going through her pregnancy alone and the shock of delivering two babies instead of one, she really needed to be catered to.

Her transformation took Marcel's breath away. He was so used to seeing her in sweats and baggy clothes that he forgot just how sexy she could be. Standing to his feet, he admired her with lust. Unable to keep his eyes off her as she walked towards him. Caught in a trance, his eyes danced with hers until she approached the table. "You look incredible," he said licking his lips, anticipating their lovemaking later on.

She looked away, blushing. Something about the way he looked at her. His penetrating eyes brought back old feelings that she thought were gone. "Thank you. I feel incredible too. That was exactly what I needed."

Gently, he grabbed her hand, kissing it tenderly. His soft lips brushed against the back of her hand sending shivers down her spine and moisture to her pelvic region.

Marcel moved aside so Natalia could slide into the booth. This was the same booth they sat at nearly a year ago. "I hope you don't mind. I already ordered."

"I see some things never change."

The last thing Marcel wanted was to upset her. "I can call the waiter back if you want to order for yourself."

"I was just joking. I'm cool." The statement came out with assurance. However, she was anything but. Marcel had her feeling nervous. The same way he did when they first met.

The waiter came over sitting down the bottle of wine after filling both glasses. "I'll be right back with your appetizers." He waited for a brief second to see if there was anything else Marcel wanted before he excused himself.

"I bet you're wondering why I brought you back here. Why we're sitting at the same booth as before."

Put My Name On It

That's exactly what Natalia was thinking. Not saying a word, she just smiled and sipped on her wine.

The look on her face told him that's exactly what she was thinking. "I wanted to recreate the night we met. Do things right. Feel me?" He slid his fingers between hers. "I feel like I let you down last time. So tonight is all about showing you that I'm not the man you think I am. I want to redeem myself."

Reminiscing about the past turned Natalia's mood sour. "You just had to bring that up, right?" She snatched her hand from his, attempting to get up, but Marcel wouldn't move so she could get out.

As soon as she stood, he gently pulled her into his lap. "Let me be there for you and the kids. I know I messed up. I know that, baby," he said, whispering in her ear. His warm breath tickled her ear lobe. "All I'm asking is for a second chance." Overwhelmed with lust, he nuzzled her neck, taking in her sweet scent.

Tears came to Natalia's eyes. She hated how easily he tugged at her heart, making her feel vulnerable. "Let me go. I'm not trying to hear your bullshit again." She wiggled in his lap, trying to get away. "I fell for it the last time. It won't happen again."

"It's not bullshit." She felt good in his arms. He wasn't about to let her get away this time. "I mean every word. I missed you. I thought about you every day while we were apart. Now that I have you again, I'm never letting you go."

111

Natalia thought about him every day too. But the hurt deep inside of her wouldn't let her express that to him. "You made a fool out of me," she said, blinking back more tears. Her eyes dropped to the hardwood floor in embarrassment. "You made me feel special that night and took it all away in the morning. How do you think that made me feel?"

Marcel felt her pain. His heart was breaking too. The thought of leaving her behind pregnant and alone made him sick to his stomach. Never in a million years would he have made such a sucka ass move. Still, he couldn't deny that's exactly what he did. No sense playing the excuse game. The only option was for him to man-up and own it. The fact is, he got her pregnant and now they have two beautiful babies who needed them both.

"I'm so sorry," he said with his hand rested on her bottom and his chin on her shoulder. "What can I do to make things right? Just say it. I'll do whatever it takes. Anything you say. I just want to put this behind us so we can move forward together, as a family."

Natalia listened carefully as he spoke. She knew for sure that she loved him. And she couldn't deny their sexual attraction. "Anything," she whispered seductively, touching his neatly trimmed facial hair. Her wine glass was now empty. Feeling a buzz from the wine clouded her judgment. Her extra flirty behavior was a direct result of drinking way too fast out of nervousness.

"Anything," he whispered back, his lips inches from hers. His eyes traveled to her shiny kissable lips to the racy outfit hugging her body to her pretty toes in the red stilettos. The heat from her body settled right in his lap, giving him a full-blown erection. He moved his hand to rest on her inner thigh, caressing her tender flesh.

The hardness poking Natalia's bottom was a clear indication that Marcel was in heat just as much as she was. She turned around so that she was almost face to face with him. "Surprise me," she said, enticing him even more.

Natalia was horny. That didn't mean she hadn't forgotten what Marcel did. Those memories were imprinted in her thoughts, but it didn't change the fact that she lusted after him. Only Marcel had the magic touch to satisfy her itch.

Knowing what was going to happen next, Marcel caught the attention of the waiter as he passed by, changing their order to take out. The waiter rushed away and came back within moments with their food in neatly packed containers. Marcel paid the bill and left a gracious tip.

Hand in hand, they exited the restaurant like two long lost lovers.

Chapter 17

"I've been waiting a long time to have you," Marcel said, whipping into a parking space right in front of Natalia's house. He jumped out of the car and began walking briskly towards the door. All he could think about was a much needed release. His *Johnson* was hard enough to fuck her right there on the front lawn.

Natalia felt the urgency as well. However, when she tried to unfasten her seatbelt, she couldn't get out. "Wait!" she yelled out the window as Marcel quickly approached her front porch. "I can't get out." She pulled on the seatbelt repeatedly without it coming undone.

Marcel was standing on her porch ready to open the door with his spare key when Natalia call out to him. Looking over his shoulder, he noticed that she was still in the car. He sighed before jogging back. All he wanted was the hot sweaty sex that he'd been dreaming about. "What's wrong?"

"I can't get out," she responded, pulling on the seatbelt once again.

Marcel opened the door and leaned into the car. Covering her body with his, he tried to unfasten her. He jerked on the seatbelt, repeatedly. Still, he couldn't free her. "What the hell is going on? This shit ain't never happened before." He yanked even harder on the seatbelt, obviously pissed off. "This is messing up my damn flow." He kept pulling on the seatbelt, but it wouldn't come loose.

"Ouch!" Natalia smacked his hand. "You're hurting me."

"This car is too damn expensive to have a defective seatbelt." Marcel gave it one last jerk before giving up, staring at her huffing and puffing. This fucked up his whole plan. As horny as he was, he could have kicked the dashboard in. *I finally get her where I want her and this shit happens.*

Trying to free her caused friction between them. He was positioned across her lap with his dick lined up perfectly. His erection poked against her inner thigh, very close to her vagina, making her nature rise. Natalia's breathing became labored. The more he pulled, the more his body shifted. She felt his manhood poking against her swollen clit.

"I'ma cut the damn thing," Marcel said, finally giving up. Beyond disgusted, he turned on his side, falling into a groove between her legs. He patted himself down wondering what the hell he did with his pocket knife. "No matter what, I'll get you out." He looked at her finally noticing the sensual stare.

She reached out, touching his growing erection.

Princess Diamond

Marcel stopped looking for his pocket knife. "Fuck this seatbelt shit." He glanced at Natalia to see if she was down.

She was totally on board slightly parting her legs. "Give it to me then," she purred.

No more words needed to be exchanged. The sexual energy between them spoke volumes.

Marcel wasted no time leaning her seat all the way back. He climbed into the car and closed the door behind him. The tight space in the car provided the perfect amount of comfort for their unmasked desire.

Natalia opened her legs as wide as she could, resting one foot on the dashboard and the other against the car door. Despite being strapped in the confines of a seat belt, she found a way to pull him even closer, freeing his manhood. "Enter me."

Marcel entered her with his thick penis in one thrust. "Damn you feel good. I've been dreaming about being in this pussy for months."

"Ah! Me too," Natalia moaned, gripping his ass so he would go deeper. Her eyes fluttered at the depth of his penetration. She savored the moment of how good he actually felt. "I love how you fit inside of me. Oh...Oh...Oh...It's sooooo good."

"I swear your pussy is the best."

Marcel continued to squirm around in the small space until he was hitting her spot just right. Being inside of Natalia made him weak. He was on the verge of shooting hot cum which made him regret not having sex in a long time. Her sweet pussy had him on the threshold of busting a nut. He kissed her lips, wondering how much longer he could hold back his load.

"Damn, this pussy," he whispered, nibbling on her ear.

"Oh! Yes! Right There! Marcel, fuck me, baby!" Natalia closed her eyes tight and screamed out in ecstasy. "I'm...about... to... cum." Her freshly manicured nails clawed at his seats as she wiggled her hips underneath him. "Oooooooooooooooooh." Her vaginal walls contracted, squeezing his manhood as she came.

Natalia's wild upward thrusts nearly drove him Marcel insane. It was a hard pounding that rocked the car back and forth. Seconds after her orgasm, Marcel let out a deep throaty groan before he released loads of sperm.

"Shit, that was good," Marcel said, trying to catch his breath.

"Yes, it was," Natalia said still trying to catch hers too.

They stayed in each other's arms for several minutes before they both regained their composure.

Finally Marcel got off of her, opening the car door, stepping out. He used a wipe from the glove compartment to clean himself off before zipping his pants.

Just like magic, the moment Natalia tried to get out, the seatbelt unsnapped freeing her from its grip.

Princess Diamond

They both laughed thinking the same thing.

We were going at it so rough the seatbelt came loose.

Chapter 18

"Come inside." Natalia stood in the doorway begging Marcel with longing eyes to have a nightcap with her. She was feeling the sex they just had and looking forward to getting some more of his good loving. Waking up next to him would be the icing on the cake since she didn't get to experience that with him the first time. All she wanted was the happy ending to a beautiful night.

The offer was tempting to Marcel. Of course he wanted to come inside and finish beating her pussy up. The thought of waking up next to her in the morning made his dick hard again. His body told him yes, but his mind told him no. After pondering the decision, he decided against it. The last thing he wanted to tell Natalia was no, but it was in his best interest to play things cool. He just won her back and he planned on keeping her. Coming inside this soon could mess things up, just like last time.

Leaning in, he gave her a sweet kiss good-bye. "Some other time, ok?" He looked her in the eye, kindly touching her face.

"Ok," Natalia said, pouting. She really wanted him to stay. "You sure you gotta go?"

"Yeah, but I got you next time."

"Promise?"

Marcel kissed her again. "That's my word."

"You better or that's your ass." Natalia still wasn't satisfied with his answer, but she respected it.

"You have my word."

She crossed her arms over her chest like a spoiled brat. "Whatever."

"I'm saying, I got you."

"You better."

"I will. Trust me." Marcel hugged her tight for re-assurance.

Natalia wanted to trust him. "I just don't want to be hurt again."

"And you won't be. I'm telling you, I'm all yours," he said, looking at her with loving eyes.

Natalia stared Marcel down before he loosened his embrace, walking away. He strutted toward his car, feeling great about the night because things went exactly as planned. He finally conquered and she was back on board.

As he approached his car, he looked back once more just to see if Natalia was still standing there watching. Sure enough, she was in the doorway burning a hole in the back, upset about his departure.

Put My Name On It

Look at her sexy ass pouting. I got her right where I want her.

Marcel blew Natalia a kiss as he drove away feeling like the luckiest man in the world. As he was about to pull off her block, his cell rang.

"Hello," he answered wondering who in the hell was calling him so late.

"Hey," Mia said on the other end. "You got a minute?"

"Not really, but what's up?"

"I need you to come into the office."

"Tonight?"

"Yeah, these papers need to be signed so I can turn them into the lawyer right away."

"Can't that wait til morning?" The last thing Marcel wanted to do was drive downtown.

"Not really. They were supposed to be returned yesterday. I thought you were coming in this morning but you never showed."

"Nah, I never said I was coming in."

"Well, right now, that's irrelevant. I have to drop them off tonight. They were due two days ago."

The phone was silent.

"Marcel, it's very important," Mia stated bluntly. "We're talking about millions of dollars."

Marcel sighed loudly revealing his disappointment. "Ok, you made your point. I'm on my way."

Princess Diamond

"Thank you," Mia said politely. "I'll see you short-ly."

Hanging up in disgust, Marcel pressed down on the accelerator. The drive downtown was definitely out of his way, messing everything up. He was trying to prove how responsible he was and this unexpected de-tour was going to make him late picking up the twins. The last thing he wanted to be was irresponsible with his children. Natalia would be turned off immediately, deeming him unfit. That would ruin all the progress that he just made.

Driving faster than usual, Marcel made a poor choice proceeding through the intersection on a yellow light. It turned red as soon as he crossed the busy street, making him run the light.

Out of nowhere, a police car appeared followed by the familiar sounds of a siren.

Whoop! Whoop! Whoop! Whoop! Whoop!

Looking in the review mirror, Marcel saw the po-lice car tailing him. *Dayum. I don't need this bullshit right now. Why the hell do they have to be filling a fuckin quota tonight? Fuck!*

Pissed off, he jerked the wheel hard, pulling over to the side. The quicker he cooperated and got his tick-et, the faster he would be on his merry way. Signing those papers and picking his kids up were his only con-cern.

Put My Name On It

"License and registration." The officer said the moment he approached the car, shining the flashlight in Marcel's face, blinding him.

Seriously, I'm not in the mood for this shit tonight. "I know I ran the light officer," Marcel said, reaching for his wallet. "Can you just give me the ticket so I can be on my way? I'm kinda in a hurry."

"License and registration," the officer demanded for a second time.

"Sure, Officer, just a moment." Marcel reached in his pocket, noticing that his wallet wasn't there. He began to pat himself down trying to think where it could be. Remembering the rump he just had with Natalia, it was a strong possibility that his wallet was on the floor or under the seat. "I'm not sure where my license is, Officer. But if you allow me to look around inside my car, I might be able to find it."

"That won't be necessary," the officer responded with an attitude. "Can you step out of the car?"

Marcel was clueless as to what the problem was. "Wait a minute. This is just one big misunderstanding." Marcel continued to wreck his brain, trying to figure out where his wallet could be.

Just then two more police cars pulled up.

Four more officers approached them with their weapons drawn. "Get out of the car, now!" one of them shouted.

Awww, shit! Here we g with this bullshit.

123

Princess Diamond

Marcel didn't know why the five officers were about to detain him. Something told him not to go against the grain and do what they said or there was a possibility he might make the front page news as a statistic. All he could think about were the twins and how they could be fatherless if he made the wrong move. Had they not been born, who knows how this would have turned out. His natural instinct was to react violently.

"Ok. Ok. I'm getting out the car now." Slowly opening the car door, he put one foot out and held his hands high in the air so they could see them. "See, I don't have anything to hide. Just don't shoot." Using precise and careful movements so the officers weren't alarmed, Marcel cautiously extracted himself from his vehicle.

The five officers rushed him at once, giving him several body blows before they wrestled him to the ground with extensive force, handcuffing him.

"You have the right to remain silent...."

That was the last thing Marcel heard before he blacked out.

Chapter 19

Natalia wanted to yell out to Marcel as he drove away. Standing on the porch, she hoped he would turn around and come back. Seeing his taillights disappear brought back those same rejected feelings from the last time he sexed her like crazy and left. Tears came to her eyes. She got the funniest feeling that he was going to pull same disappearing act as before.

No, we have something special now. I don't think he would do me like that again. Or would he?

She dismissed the negative thoughts, knowing that he cared deeply for her. They were a family now. Last time, they hardly knew each other. This time, he was fully aware of what he was getting himself into.

Besides he practically begged me to take him back. I need to stop trippin. I shouldn't have anything to worry about.

She walked inside closing the door. Feeling very lonely and overcome with emotion, she leaned back against the door missing him even more. Her heart overflowed and it was at that very moment, she realized how much she truly loved him. Not because he was famous or because he was her kid's father. It had nothing to do with the fact that he was the best sex she ever had either.

She loved him because he gave her butterflies every time she saw him. She loved the way he looked at her with desire. She loved how considerate he was when they spent time together. She loved the way he paid attention to the little things that she liked. And most importantly, she knew that he loved her. Not only did he show it, but he said it too. Marcel was the type of man that she could spend the rest of her life with. He was definitely a keeper.

Grabbing her keys, she raced out the door, determined to go after her man. *I need to tell him how I really feel.*

Making it as far as the front porch, she quickly changed her mind, retreating back inside.

I am going to look like a fool once again. If he wanted to stay, he would have. I gave him every opportunity to say yes, and he decided against it. I guess I'll just have to wait this out and see what happens.

Hurt and confused, she rushed upstairs throwing herself across the queen-sized bed. Her feet dangled over the edge as she shed many tears on her over-sized pillow.

I can't keep doing this with him. It hurts too bad. No matter how much I love him, I can't allow him to have this much control over me.

Put My Name On It

It was morning before Natalia knew it. Drowsy and tired, she rolled out of bed knowing that she couldn't spend all day sleeping. Stretching and standing to her feet, she checked her phone to see if Marcel called. Nothing. Rolling her eyes at the ceiling, she placed her cell back on the night stand.

He was supposed to drop the kids off by now.

Walking into the bathroom, she saw how crying made her face look puffy and wrinkled. There was no way Marcel could see her like this. After taking a quick shower, she washed her face and applied just enough make up to hide her true emotions.

It was almost noon. He would have been here by now. I hope things are ok.

The nervousness in her stomach told her that something was wrong. She was sure that Marcel would have dropped the kids off by now. She tried to relax and wait for him to show up, but her instincts wouldn't let her. Picking up the phone, she dialed his home number. No answer. She dialed his cell. It went straight to voicemail.

What the hell?

Those same old feelings resurfaced and rejection stared her in the face.

Don't tell me he did it again?

She was about to try his cell again when her phone rang. It was her grandmother asking her to come and get the kids. Apparently Marcel never showed up.

Princess Diamond

Oh, no he didn't forget about my babies. That's number one on my list of mess ups. He better have a damn good excuse for this.

Natalia was heated.

Leaving me is one thing, but leaving the kids is not acceptable. There's no excuse for that. I'm done with his ass for good. He keeps doing this shit because I allow him too. I can't have my babies in the middle of this nonsense. What kind of mother would I be?

Natalia hung up the phone with a real attitude. She wanted to strangle Marcel. She grabbed the first outfit she saw in her closet, a tracksuit. She needed to get to her grandmother's house as soon as possible, knowing that the kids had been there all night.

That woman is too old to be handling two babies overnight.

Within minutes, she was dressed and ready to leave. Charging out the front door towards her car, she tripped over something that appeared to be left near her steps. After nearly falling on the concrete face first, she turned around to see what tripped her. Analyzing the object for a moment, she decided to pick it up.

Why in the hell is Marcel's wallet on my front porch? Damn he is careless and real unreliable. I can't believe I even considered spending the rest of my life with him. What a loser!

Chapter 20

Natalia's feelings were at an all-time high—an emotional rollercoaster. She had thoughts of destroying everything in the house. Balling up her fists, she threw air punches. After fighting an invisible being for a few minutes, she collapsed backwards onto her bed crying like a lovesick puppy.

It's been three fuckin weeks since I seen him. I should kick myself in the ass for being so damn stupid.

She went by Marcel's condo several times. Called his phone over and over. Left him numerous voicemails until it was full. No response.

I'm so sick of this shit.

Marcel's sudden disappearance caught her totally off guard. Never in a million years did she think he would pull such an act. Not after the way he made promise after promise to get his family back. She was sure that he would have followed through with good intentions.

As if Marcel's unexpected disappearance wasn't bad enough, Natalia hadn't slept more than two hours a night for the last three weeks. As soon as she picked the kids up from her grandmother's house, they got sick.

It seemed like the children were taking turns keeping Natalia up all night. If she got one child down for the night, the other child was in agony crying. Marcelius got sick first with an ear infection. She stayed up with him for a week straight. By the time he calmed down, Marcelina got sick with a cold.

Dealing with two sick babies for three weeks straight was the worse. Natalia was totally burned out. Mentally and physically. She was agitated, angry, and unable to keep any food down. Not only was she throwing up, but she was weak and frustrated. If there was a time that she needed Marcel, this would definitely be it.

Dragging herself out of bed, she sat on the edge collecting her thoughts. Her eyes burned and she had bags from a lack of sleep. As bad as she wanted to crawl back into bed, she couldn't. The kids were overdue for their checkup. There was no way she could put it off any longer, especially with them both still being ill.

Walking out of her room into the kid's nursery, she looked into their cribs. Watching them sleep peacefully dissolved her anger a little.

I love my little angels. Getting my act together isn't just for me, but for my kids too. They are depending on me. I have no choice but to be the best mother for them since they have no father.

Put My Name On It

Both babies were up in the middle of the night crying. After pacifying them with a warm bath, they finally went to sleep. Taking advantage of their exhaustion, Natalia bathed and dressed them ahead of time so she wouldn't have to wake them for their doctor's appointment in the morning.

Cradling Marcelius in her arms, she couldn't help but notice how much he looked like Marcel. A rush of emotion dominated her as she thought about her son not having a father in his life. Determined not to cry, she quickly strapped him in his car seat, praying that he stayed sleep the whole time.

The moment she picked up Marcelina, her eyes popped open. Natalia just knew that she was about to scream so she pushed her pacifier into her mouth to suppress it. At first, Marcelina wouldn't take it, spitting it out. It seemed like a battle trying to take it. Rocking her gently, the baby finally closed her eyes sucking on it. Natalia held her daughter close until she went back to sleep. When she was sure that she wouldn't wake back up, she placed her in the pink car seat, sitting adjacent to her brother.

It was more than a task getting both babies downstairs, putting them in the double stroller, and pushing them to the car. Once she was at the car, she unhooked each child's car seat placing them securely in the backseat. Before getting into the car, she struggled putting the heavy stroller in the trunk.

Princess Diamond

At first, she was against the six hundred dollar stroller when Marcel bought it. That amount of money spent on a stroller just seemed like a waste. However, it was times like these that she was very appreciative that he didn't listen to her. That stroller was top of the line and it came in handy on days like this when she was all by herself caring for twins.

I'm so pissed at Marcel right now. He should be here. Lugging these heavy ass babies around is like a second job.

Natalia stood on the side of the car rubbing her temples, calming her nerves. Just thinking about Marcel was about to bring on another crying spell. And she was too exhausted to cry right now. Being sleep deprived, tired took precedent over tears. If she was going to use the last of her energy, it wasn't going to be to crying over her kid's father.

From the tightness of her face, she knew she looked a hot mess from the lack of sleep and constant crying. Sighing heavily, she shifted her mindset back to the task at hand. Her goal was to get the babies to their appointment and then come back home and get some rest. Hopefully, by the time they returned, it would be time to administer both babies their medicine, assuring her a few hours of much needed sleep.

Natalia couldn't stand bringing the kids to the doctor. It was always an adventure. The parking garage stayed over crowded. It was never enough seats available in the waiting room. Some kid was always coughing spreading germs.

Usually, she avoided this madness because she had early morning visits. But this time it was in the afternoon. The kids had an emergency follow up due to their illnesses. She missed the first appointment so she had to be squeezed in. This was the first available time.

I hope these people aren't off the chain up in here. I'm not in the mood for no drama. My patience is short as hell right now. Today would be the day I catch a case. God be with me. Please! I have no problem beating someone down.

Natalia found a cramped up seat in the far left corner of the office. Her nerves were shot as she sat wedged in between two extra talkative teens. The nonstop chatter and excessive giggling about nothing had her on the verge of poppin off. Every time the nurse walked out, she prayed that the twins were called. The only good thing about this visit so far was the twins were still asleep.

They won't be sleep for long if I don't get away from these chatty ass broads next to me.

"Girl, do you see who's on the cover of this magazine?"

"Un-uh, girl, who?"

"Ya man, Urbane." Natalia's ears perked up when she heard them mention Marcel's stage name.

"Fa real, what it say about my boo?"

133

Princess Diamond

The girl on Natalia's left skimmed the article. "Ok, listen to this. It says, Marcel Pisano aka Urbane was born to an Italian American mother and an African American father. Growing up in the mean streets of Harlem, he managed to stay out of trouble by writing songs. While others were hanging out, he was sitting in his bedroom window or on the fire escape, dreaming of being famous one day."

Natalia sighed loudly attracting the attention of both girls. They briefly looked at her crazy before going back to the magazine.

The girl continued to read, "Anyways, listen to this. He is single, but recently welcomed the birth of twins."

Oh, hell no! I know his ass didn't tell this magazine he was single. This lying muthafucka. This is why I'm done with this ass. I should have never fucked around with him.

Natalia began tapping her foot against the carpet to calm her nerves. It was bad enough Marcel was gone. She didn't know where the hell he was or when he would be back. Adding insult to injury, she had to sit in the doctor's office and listen to two groupie teens rundown his life story.

"Marcelius and Marcelina Pisano," the nurse called out.

Natalia practically jumped out of her seat. "Right here." She waved her hand so the nurse would see her.

"Wait a minute," one of the teens said. "Did you hear them kid's names?"

"I did," the other teen said with a ghetto flare. "Do you think that's Urbane's kids? You know he lives here in Chicago."

"I know right."

Natalia could feel their eyes on her back as she pushed the babies towards the nurse.

"They prolly are his kids. That would explain why she was sucking her teeth and acting all strange and whatnot."

"Ok! Sighing all loud and giving us the screw face."

The teens giggled loudly.

Natalia wanted to put them both on blast.

I want to confront them so bad, but I can't stoop to their level. I know the truth. I don't have to prove my-self. Urbane, Marcel, or whatever the hell he goes by can't change the fact that these babies are his.

"Right this way," the nurse said, cutting her eyes at the teens. "How are you, today?"

"Tired and sleepy," Natalia answered truthfully. "Having two sick babies has to be the worse."

"I totally understand. I have twins too. And they always seemed to get sick at the same time. But it does get better as they get older."

Natalia gave a half-hearted smile. "If I make it to that point. It doesn't even seem possible right now."

"It'll get better. I promise you. It will."

"Natalia, how are you?" Dr. Meska asked. His office was adjacent to the children's doctor. Having both doctors in the same office was convenient. This is one of the reasons why she endured the madness.

"I'm fine, Dr. Meska. How are you?"

"Very well. Thank you for asking." Dr. Meska peeked in the stroller at Marcelina and smiled. Then, he directed his attention to Marcelius who was in the nurse's arms being weighed. "These kids get cuter and cuter every time I see them."

The compliment put a much needed smile on Natalia's face. "Thank you. They are my heart."

"Hey, while I have you here in the office, we can do your six week checkup."

Natalia's smile turned into a frown immediately. "Six week checkup? That's next week, right?"

Dr. Meska gave Natalia a confused look before he stared at the chart in his hand. "No, actually, it's overdue."

"Are you sure?" Natalia asked, wrecking her brain. She could have sworn the date hadn't passed.

"Dr. Meska is right," the nurse chimed in. "Cause these cute little babies are almost nine weeks old."

The more she thought about it, she realized she was so consumed with the babies' well-being that she totally spaced her own appointment. "I apologize. I can make another appointment before I leave."

Put My Name On It

Dr. Meska looked at his chart again. "Well, if you'd like I can get you in now. I have two cancellations. That way you don't have to reschedule." Dr. Meska saw the skeptical look on Natalia's face. "You know, since you're already here. Might as well get it over with, right?"

"I can keep up with the kids for you," the nurse offered.

"I don't know." Natalia wasn't worried about leaving the kids. She just wasn't ready to climb up on the table with her coochie exposed. "Maybe rescheduling would be better."

"Nonsense," the nurse reassured her. "Now, there are plenty of doctors and nurses here. We care for babies all the time. The kids will be fine. Go take care of yourself. You can't care for your kids if you're not well."

Natalia looked away from the nurse's encouraging face to Dr. Meska. "Ok, why not," she finally agreed.

Natalia kissed both kids and followed behind Dr. Meska through the double doors that separated his side of the office.

"Miranda," Dr. Meska said to one of his nurses. "Can you take care of her? Also, I want urine and blood samples."

"Sure, Dr. Meska," Miranda said, jumping up from the front desk at his request.

"Why urine and blood samples?" Natalia asked.

137

"Well, you said you have been extremely tired. And I know the babies have been keeping you up, but I just want to make sure everything else is in order. No infections or anything." Dr. Meska gave her a reassuring smile. "There's nothing to worry about. It's routine for all my new mothers. Your health is my main concern."

"I understand, Dr. Meska."

"Alright then, I'll see you in a few."

After Miranda finished obtaining blood and samples, she led Natalia to an examination room. "Get undressed from the waist down and Dr. Meska will be with you in a few minutes."

Natalia rolled her eyes and began undressing. *This is such a headache. I don't want any more kids.*

Dr. Meska entered the room with his usual cheerful demeanor. "Are you ready?" he asked, putting the rubber gloves on.

"As ready as I'll ever be," Natalia replied, trying not to flinch from being in the stirrups. She hated getting pelvic examines.

Four minutes later, Dr. Meska scooted his chair away from her. "I'll be back once you get dressed."

Natalia noticed the weird expression on his face. "Is everything alright?"

He gave her a forced smiled. "We'll talk once you're dressed. When I come back, I'll have your lab results." He patted her knee for reassurance before he left.

What if Marcel gave me something? Or if I have a tumor. Ohmigod! What if it's cancer?

Natalia slowly rose to her feet to get dressed. On the verge of tears, she took a few deep breathes.

Calm down and hear what the man has to say. You don't even know the news yet and you're already freaking out.

By the time, Dr. Meska came back into the room Natalia was pacing back and forth. "What's wrong with me, Doc? Am I going to die? How long do I have to live?"

Dr. Meska chuckled. "Calm down. You're not about to die."

"What did you find then? And be straight with me. I know something is wrong."

Dr. Meska shook his head and laughed again. "Looks like you're expecting again."

Natalia blinked rapidly. "Excuse me?" She was prepared to hear anything but that.

Dr. Meska's bright smile slowly faded. "That would explain some of the symptoms you were telling me about. I had a suspicion but I wanted to be sure. Congratulations."

"I can't believe this," Natalia mumbled.

"It's more common than you think."

Natalia just stared at him in awe. She didn't know what to think or how to feel.

"I wrote you a prescription to fill. The nurse will give them to you when you get the kids."

Natalia left the doctor's office in a state of shock. Expecting a routine visit, she was stunned to find out that she was pregnant again. After strapping both kids in the backseat, she sat behind the wheel in a trance. Dr. Meska's words replayed in her mind. *Looks like you're expecting again.*

The reality of having another baby sunk in. The thought of raising three kids with no father broke her heart. The tears that she had been holding back started to fall. Within minutes, she was sobbing uncontrollably. The hurt was unbearable.

I can't believe Marcel got me pregnant again. And just like before, he isn't anywhere to be found. How could I allow this to happen to me twice? The twins won't even be a year old when this baby is born.

After much thought, having another baby was out of the question. It was a struggle just keeping up with the twins. There was no way she could be a single mother of three.

Reluctantly, she picked up her cell making a call to the clinic. It broke her heart to go this route, but she didn't see any other way. Getting an abortion was her only option.

Chapter 21

"Yo, what happened to my phone call?"

Marcel had been in a cell by himself for a few days. Prior to that, he was in the hospital. The beating the police put on him was so bad they had to rush him through emergency instead of booking him in the county jail.

When the doctor asked about his injuries, of course, the officers lied. Marcel was unconscious and handcuffed to a bed for weeks with survelliance. The hospital staff had specific instructions to alert police officials as soon as he woke up.

Nearly three weeks later, he woke up in great condition despite being beaten into a coma. His bruises were almost healed except for a small mark on his face. He didn't suffer any brain damage or memory loss, which was nothing short of a miracle.

"Quiet down over there," the rookie officer on duty said.

Marcel couldn't see the officer, but he knew he was a brother by the way he spoke. This was the first time he'd had a brother on duty. He planned on taking full advantage of it. "Listen Officer, there's been a mistake. You have the wrong man. I didn't commit a crime."

The officer didn't think twice about what Marcel just said. He'd heard that excuse more than a hundred times. "That's what they all say, young brutha."

"I'm serious, Officer. On some real shit, my life is too good to do anything stupid. I'm sure you heard of me. I go by the stage name Urbane."

The officer laughed hard at the inmate's desperate attempt at freedom. "Quit bullshitting, nicca. Now, you really reaching. Don't make this harder than what it has to be."

Marcel knew he had to say something back to provoke a conversation. "I promise you, I am, Officer. I lost my wallet. That's why I don't have any ID. The night I was picked up, I was speeding. I admit, I did run the light, but I didn't commit whatever crime they claim I did. I was with my girl and my kids the whole day." He could tell he piqued the officer's attention.

"You ain't no damn Urbane. Get the fuck outta here. I'd know him if I saw him."

"Come check me out then. See for yourself."

"I ain't gon lie, you do sound like him, though."

"That's cuz I am."

The chair squeaked. "Man, if you got me up for nothing, you're going to be sorry. I'm tired as shit right now from working a double. I ain't got time for the dumb-dumb."

After listening to the man behind the bars talk a good game, the officer was curious. He had to get up and see if he was really Urbane. Walking into plain view, he examined the man caged up. Beyond the scar on his cheek and the dirty clothes, he did look just like the superstar. "If you really Urbane, spit something then."

Without hesitation, Marcel began rapping his latest song *Hot like Fire.* Using his thumb as a microphone he broke out into his signature dance. He performed as if he was at Madison Square Garden in front of hundreds of people. Going hard, Marcel gave a stellar performance, rapping for his freedom.

By the time he finished, the officer was bobbing his head, moving from side to side, and rapping along with him. Marcel wasn't stupid. He knew this was his last chance to break free. If he didn't utilize this moment, he may never get out.

The officer's eyes lit up with appreciation. "Man, I thought you was lying." He gave a throaty chuckle. "You really that nicca Urbane. I can't fuckin believe it."

Marcel quickly switched gears. "You think I can still get that phone call?"

"Hell yeah! But you gotta give me an autograph though. It's for my wife and kids. They love you, man.

143

My son got all your albums. His mind is going to be blown when I tell him that I met you. This is so wild." The officer unlocked the cell. "Say, when you doing another concert, man?"

Marcel followed the officer over to his desk. He was so happy to finally be getting his long awaited phone call. "I'm not sure. But I'ma look out for you. I got tickets for you and your family. I'll fly you out, set up the hotel stay, and everything. All expenses on me."

"You fa real? Straight up? Don't be lying."

"That's my word."

The overweight officer was so happy he began doing an old school two-step. "Watch out, now. Wait until I tell my partnas. They gonna flip." His grin was so wide Marcel could see all the gaps between his teeth.

"Yo, you looked out for me. I gotta look out for you."

The officer stared at him like he was his favorite meal. "See, that's what I'm talking about, man." He was in awe of Marcel "You know what, you alright with me. I don't care what nobody say. You the shit."

Although Marcel had been through hell and back, he couldn't help but laugh at the overweight officer's theatrical persona. It reminded him of some of the cats he used to watch out the window back home in Harlem.

Chapter 22

Marcel stood in front of his lawyer going berserk. "What the hell took you so fuckin long? I placed that call to you hours ago. You know they got me hemmed up. And you strolling your ass up in here like every thing's all good."

Anger consumed Marcel's whole body. He was heated because he couldn't understand why this bullshit was happening to him. He wanted to know why he was locked up when he was innocent. "What the hell were you doing all that damn time? On the strength of that hefty retainer, you should have got back at me within minutes. And on my mama, it's taking everything in me not to jump on your ass right now."

Marvin Kultz had been dealing with Marcel for years so he was used to seeing all sides of him. In this situation, he couldn't blame Marcel for being pissed off. Anyone who was falsely accused, spending weeks away from the world in jail for a crime they didn't commit, would respond the same way. Mr. Kultz didn't hold Marcel's hostility against him. He knew that his reputation of being a beast in the courtroom preceded him. That's why Marcel hired him. He'd been Marcel's lawyer recommended by his father since he became an overnight millionaire. So their relationship went way back and Mr. Kultz didn't intend on allowing this misunderstanding to ruin it.

Doing what he did best, Mr. Kultz intended to prove just how legendary his skills were to his most valuable client. "I assure you, Mr. Pisano, the time that I was missing in action, was in your best interest."

Mr. Kultz finally had Marcel's attention. Taking control, he pointed for Marcel to sit in front of him. "Let me fill you in."

Marcel stopped pacing back and forth, taking a hard look at him. For the first time since he entered the interrogation room, he glanced around noticing the raggedy folding table and two wobbly chairs.

Mr. Kultz kept his cool. "Please, have a seat. I'm sure you want to hear what I have to say."

Marcel shook his head with disbelief and gave Mr. Kultz a long stare before he took a seat in front of him. "Hold up." He put his hand up immediately, stopping Mr. Kultz from expressing his next thought. "Before you speak, it better be worth my time. That's all I have to say."

"I assure you, it will be." Mr. Kultz opened his briefcase, revealing the findings of Marcel's case. Taking out four documents, he placed them on the table in front of him.

Marcel wasted no time picking up the papers, reading them. The first two contained the details of his arrest and his hospitalization. According to the papers, the police arrested him because he drove the same car as the suspect. And without his license, he wasn't able to prove his identity. That's why they assumed he was the felon. The officers on duty that night used it to their advantage, stating that he resisted arrest and they had to use forcible restraint.

Reading the documents pissed Marcel off even more. He hit the shaky table so hard it almost broke in two. "I want the badge numbers to all the officers involved."

"No worries. I'm already working on your lawsuit. When I get done with them, not only will you have their badges, but you'll be a filthy rich man. And they'll be eating the same slop they served you in here."

Marcel nodded in agreement before reading the third paper that contained the identity of the man he was mistaken for. Having the same car was the only coincidence. This man looked nothing like him. And the dude had a rap sheet as long as a roll of toilet paper. "Is he is custody?"

"He's being detained as we speak."

Marcel picked up the forth paper which was a copy of his release. "So, I'm free to go?"

Mr. Kultz nodded. "Yes. Free and clear to return to your life and live as usual. This is why it took me so long to get back to you. I had to gather evidence to prove your innocence before I found a judge to sign off on your immediate release."

Marcel extended his hand to his lawyer. "Job well done, but I want to be in the loop next time."

Mr. Kultz shook his client's hand firmly with a smile, knowing he did his job very well. "I understand. But what I want you to know is you hired me to make things happen. And that's what I'm going to do. My main concern is always your best interest. When you don't hear from me, just know that I'm always taking care of business. In this case, if I stopped to fill you in, it might have cost you another night being in jail. I know that's not what you wanted. So I had no choice but to put you off and use the time I had to get you out of here."

Marcel heard Mr. Kultz loud and clear. Still, he wanted to get knee deep in his ass for leaving him on pins and needles for hours. But at the same time, the man was working the hell out of the system so he had to respect that. "Did you take care of the list of things I asked for?"

"I sure did," Mr. Kultz replied. "Everything is done just like you asked."

Put My Name On It

Marcel decided to drop his hostility. Time and time again, his lawyer has shown his ability to be the best. He wasn't about to give him a hard time for making sure he was vindicated. All the charges were dropped. He was free to go. He did a damn good job. "Thank you. I apologize for my bad attitude. This place will make the most sane individual go ape shit."

"Apology accepted. And for the record, I totally understand. You have every right to feel the way you do. I would never hold that against you. We've been in business for way too long."

They shook on it and Mr. Kultz accompanied Marcel while they processed his released.

Marcel was finally a free man. He walked out of Cook County Jail with his lawyer by his side. Words couldn't describe how irate he was. Nobody would believe the horrible mistake that had been made. And he couldn't get back the last three weeks of his life.

Chicago PD fucked up big time and he planned on making them pay dearly. But right now, suing the police department wasn't his on his mind.

He had to get back to his family. His gut was telling him that he was in the process of losing them. This disappearing act might have cost his relationship. Even though it wasn't his fault, he was sure Natalia wouldn't see it that way. It all sounds made up, which made him fear her reaction even more. She probably thought he was pulling the same bullshit as before. No matter what she thought, he wasn't going down without a fight. He was determined to get things back on track and win her back at all costs. It was time to pull out the big guns.

In a hurry, Marcel made his way home. After checking his place out and making sure nothing was missing, he got a fresh haircut, showered, and changed clothes. He knew he had to make contact with his family back in New York. They were probably worried sick. Briefly, he gave his mother the rundown and told her he loved her and would make arrangements to see her as soon as possible. Next, he called Mia, breaking down what happened and what she needed to hookup for the kind officer who helped him out.

Finally, he called Cash, who was speechless. The situation was so random that it sounded like Marcel made it up. Of course, Cash knew his best friend wouldn't tell no lie like that. Marcel has always been truthful with Cash. They had no secrets. And there was no reason for Cash to start doubting him now. He knew Marcel would never create some estranged story to save face. If Marcel said that's what happened, then Cash was rockin with it. And he was on board with whatever Marcel needed to get his life back in order.

Marcel inquired about Natalia and the kids. He wanted to get a feel for her mood. That's when Cash repeated what Karen said—that Natalia was pregnant again and she was on her way to get an abortion as they spoke.

Put My Name On It

Marcel was hurt. He was so shocked to hear the news that hung up on Cash by mistake. *I'll get at him later. Natalia is my first priority. I can't have her aborting my seed.*

Grabbing the keys to his new whip, Marcel ran out of his condo in an attempt to stop Natalia from making a huge mistake. He knew the only reason why she was having an abortion was because of his absence. Had he been there for her like he promised, she wouldn't even be considering it.

I hope I'm not too late.

Marcel pulled off his block like a bat out of hell. Pushing his new sports car to the limit, he turned corners like a maniac. Barely stopping at the stop signs. *Fuck the pigs. If they see me, they'll have the chase of their lives. I'm not stopping this time. They can holla at me when I get to the clinic.* His plan was to put an end to this nonsense with Natalia, once and for all.

Chapter 23

Natalia pulled away from the curb at high speed, cutting off the car coming down the street. Her mind was so gone that she never even noticed the car speeding towards her. The driver pumped his brakes just in time. Two seconds more and he would have been sitting in her back seat. Enraged, he honked his horn and flipped her off before cussing her out.

Oblivious to the wreck she nearly caused, Natalia never saw the theatrics going on in the car behind her. She kept on driving blinded by her tears and stuck on her current situation.

The abortion lingered in her mind nonstop. Terminating her pregnancy seemed so easy when she made the appointment. Having the procedure seemed like it would solve her problem. But the more she thought about it, the more she began to doubt if getting rid of her baby was really the answer. Deep down inside, she knew her real issue was a broken heart.

Now that she was on her way to the appointment, she wasn't so sure about the procedure. If she kept the baby, she would still have three babies in diapers. All under a year old. She'd still be a single mother of three struggling to provide for them.

I can't even take care of the two I got without going half crazy. Not to mention the financial hardship of another child. Why did I allow Marcel to do this to me again? Every time we have sex, I get pregnant. I should have known better.

She knew that whatever she decided to do, she'd have to live with that decision for the rest of her life. There would be no turning back. After pondering the decision over and over again, she finally made up her mind. Her hand rested on her stomach. She really wanted to keep her baby, but it didn't seem possible.

I'm sorry, but I can't keep you.

After breaking down once more, she finally dried her eyes and reapplied her makeup in between traffic stops.

I'll put all my effort into the two kids I already have. Give them the love of two parents. I want them to have the best. They deserve that much.

Turning onto the expressway, she noticed a red sports car speeding behind her.

Who the hell is this fool driving like a maniac? This person must be on drugs.

She couldn't see the driver's face but as fast as this person was coming made her very nervous. The car was bobbing and weaving in between lanes, barely missing cars. She knew that if she didn't get out of the way, this car was going to smash right into her. Pressing down on the accelerator, she took off. Her foot was heavy on the pedal gaining speed on the mystery driver.

The red sports car picked up speed too, making it very clear that Natalia was the intended target.

I know Marcel didn't sent one of his goons to stop me? He couldn't show up himself but he can send someone else to do his dirty work. What a punk move. Makes me want to put my foot in his ass even more.

Determined not to be caught, she showed whoever was behind the wheel that she was the boss by making an unexpected turn, getting off one exit early. *That'll show your ass. I can drive too, bastard. You better recognize.*

In a flash, Natalia's current situation didn't seem as important anymore. Getting away from this crazed driver was all she could think about. Hyped up about the chase, she whipped through the side streets as if she owned them. Within no time, she pulled up to the clinic, parking in an empty space out front.

A space out front? Maybe this is a sign that I made the right decision.

Hesitant to get out the car, she sat there for a moment allowing reality to sink in. Being in the idle car gave her more room for doubt. Fearfully, she watched pregnant women shuffle in and out the clinic. Each woman seemed to have the same disheveled look on their faces.

Who the hell am I kidding? That couldn't be further from the truth. But I gotta do what I gotta do.

After taking a few deep breaths to calm her nerves, she checked her face once again in the mirror, making sure she was still on point. *It's now or never.* She finally gained enough courage to go through with the abortion.

Cutting the car off and grabbing her purse, she attempted to get out when that same red sports car suddenly pulled up, blocking her in. The car double parked so close that she couldn't open her door.

Who is this asshole?

Looking out the window she mentally measured the space between the two cars. Whoever this was managed to leave only inches between them. If she opened the door, it would definitely put a dent in the anonymous driver's car.

See I'd be wrong if I rammed my door into this expensive ass car, fucking it up. Obviously, they don't know me cuz I'll do it.

Just as Natalia was about to make good on her threat, she realized that the mystery driver was rolling down the tinted window. Taking off his shades, Marcel revealed his face.

Natalia gasped. *I can't believe this bastard has the nerve to pop up out of nowhere. Who the hell does that?*

They engaged in a brief stare down.

Natalia rolled her eyes hard before turning away. *Fuck him! I'm still going through with it. He should have been here before now. Try and stop me, nicca. Good luck.*

Marcel sensed her attitude by the funky look on her face. *She looks like she wants to spit in my face. I'ma need a miracle to get her ass back.*

Filled with rage, Natalia thought about slapping the piss out of him. *Hell naw. He's been gone all this damn time. Now, he wants to conveniently show up in the nick of time. I don't think so. Beat it with the dumb shit.*

She wondered how he found out where she was. Then it dawned on her, it had to be Karen. She must've told Cash. Who ran his mouth to Marcel. More than likely, Marcel was probably there to stop her.

So Marcel decided to come and stop me himself instead of sending a flunky to do it. Well, bravo. It still don't' change a thing. I'm not listening to shit he got to say.

His unexpected arrival made her even more determined to follow through with the abortion.

I'm getting it done. If he's trying to stop me, let him try. He'll have to catch me first.

Put My Name On It

She snapped her neck in the opposite direction crawling across the car seat, preparing to exit through the passenger's side door.

Marcel sprang into action, anticipating Natalia's next move. Determined to stop her from going into the clinic, he leaped out his ride like he had magical powers. With stride he moved pass his car in seconds, sliding over the hood, and landing on his feet like a super hero.

Natalia looked over her shoulder and saw Marcel on her heels. She continued to hit the pavement hard with her eyes glued on the clinic doors. *I just have to get inside. Then, he can't stop me.*

"Natalia!" he yelled out. Just as he suspected, she ignored him. "Stop being brand new. Girl, you know you hear me calling your damn name." Breaking into a cool run, Marcel rushed up behind her, grabbing her by her waist, preventing her from entering the clinic. "Why you playing?"

"I'm not playing," Natalia snapped. "I'm serious."

"Look, you don't have to do this," he whispered in her ear. "I know you're doing this because of me. But I'm here now. See, I'm here."

"Get the hell off me." Natalia struggled to get out of his hold. "I'm not thinking about your ass. Let me go."

Marcel's hold was strong. "I'm never letting you go. You belong to me."

"Let me go, fa real, Marcel. I ain't got nothing to say to you."

"Why? So you can abort my seed? I'm not having it."

"Get the hell outta here with the caring father act. Where were you four weeks ago? When I really needed you, huh?"

Marcel paused briefly collecting his thoughts. He wasn't sure how he wanted to explain his false arrest. At least not right now.

Natalia mistook his silence as guilt. "Just like I thought, you on some more bullshit." Natalia snatched away from him.

She tried to sprint to the door, but just as quick, Marcel caught her again. This time by her arm. "Look, I know you're pissed off right now, but just hear me out. I have a good reason for disappearing this time."

I'd have to be real dumb bitch to listen to you right now. "Get out my way, Marcel. I don't want to hear your raggedy ass excuses. You're full of shit and you know it."

"I'm telling you, it's not an excuse."

"Seriously, if you don't let me go, I'm going to scream."

"I'll give you something to scream about, "he said in a playful manner, hoping she'd cool out.

Natalia couldn't help but grin, looking him over from head to toe. The attraction was still there even though she wanted to fight him. He was so handsome wearing casual attire. An expensive white tee, designer jean shorts, and fresh kicks. One stud earring in his ear, a diamond necklace, and an iced out watch.

As ordinary as he looked, anyone who knew real money would see his worth from miles away. Easily, he was wearing at least eighty grand.

"Hey, man," a dude said, walking up on them. He was passing by when he witnessed what he thought was Marcel man-handling Natalia. "Let the lady go. Obviously, she don't want nothing to do with you, dawg."

Natalia thought that Marcel's grip would loosen up when the stranger got involved. Nope. Just the opposite. It tightened out of anger.

Marcel took a deep breath, trying to contain his frustration. Natalia was already on his last nerve. Now, he had to deal with this rat face pedestrian who didn't know how to keep on walking. "Look, you don't know me. Why don't you keep it moving because this don't concern you."

The pedestrian stood his ground. "I can't. It looks like you're hurting the lady. I just want to make sure she's safe." The stranger stood erect and cocky as if he was ready to challenge Marcel.

"I don't care what you trying to do, back the hell up."

"I can't do that," the stranger said, poking his chest out even more.

"Mind your fuckin business, yo. I got this." Marcel wished the dude got the hint and went on his merry way before he cleaned the curb with his ass.

Noticing the vein popping out of Marcel's neck, Natalia decided to speak up before he snapped and beat the hell out of this man. It was only a matter of seconds before Marcel unleashed an ass whooping that the man would never forget. "Thank you sir for coming to my defense, but I'm fine. He's not hurting me."

"Are you sure?" the dude asked, not believing her. His eyes landed on Marcel as if he was a criminal.

"She's sure," Marcel interjected. "Now, beat it!" *Before I fuck you up!*

"Man, I wasn't talking to you. I was talking to—"

Marcel drug Natalia a few feet by the wrist, getting all up in the man's face. He played dude so close that their noses almost touched. "But I was talking to you." *Punk ass muthafucka!*

By the sick look on Marcel's face, Natalia could only imagine what he was contemplating. She stepped in between them, addressing the stranger. "Look, thank you for being concerned, but really, I'm fine."

The stranger thought Marcel was a lunatic. All he saw was an angry man holding onto a woman about to go into an abortion clinic. Ignoring Marcel's scowl, he addressed Natalia. "Miss, if he is hurting you, I'll be glad to call the cops. I'll even wait with you, if you want."

Put My Name On It

Marcel bumped Natalia out the way, nudging the dude with his shoulder, intimidating him. The stranger tried not to look so frightened, but his rapid eye movement and constant swallowing revealed just how scared he really was.

"I see, your ass don't listen. I'm trying not to fuck you up. But you're begging me to make an example out of you. I'm going to tell you one last time to take your pissy ass on. You got fifteen seconds."

The dude stepped back a little, afraid. He didn't want beef with Marcel. "Look man, I don't want no problems. I just want to help the lady if she's in trouble. That's all."

"I told you, I don't need your help," Natalia replied, trying to defuse the situation. "Believe me, I can handle myself. If he ever puts his hands on me, I'd lay his ass out."

The man looked at Natalia one last time, wondering if she was lying. *Was she covering for her man?* The look on her face told him that she was a ride or die chick. She was going to stick up for her man no matter what. Shaking his head in disgust, he walking off hoping Natalia would be alright.

Marcel burned a hole in the man's back as went in the opposite direction. Secretly, he wished the dude would come back so he could stomp a hole in his ass. "You know you almost got that man fucked up, right?"

"Whatever, Marcel, you brought all this shit on yourself."

"I'ma let that slick ass comment slide," he said, gritting his teeth. "Can we go somewhere and talk in private before I catch a case?"

"We don't have shit to talk about." Natalia was sick of his sweet nothings. There was no way she was going anywhere with him. "You and I both know that this thing, whatever we had, it just wasn't meant to be. Face it. The only thing we're good at is fucking and making babies. Everything else between us is shitty."

"It don't have to be that way. I know you think I left you, but I didn't. I was—"

"I don't care where the hell you were. Let me go."

Marcel finally let her go. She'd already caused a scene. He was sure someone was recording this bullshit and it would be all over the media as soon as they recognized who he was.

"You happy?" he asked, sick of her whining.

"Yes." Natalia thought that because she was free of his grip, she was free of him.

During the course of their argument, not only did she get farther away from the door, but a nice-size crowd had gathered. No doubt someone had probably called the cops by now. That's just how it was when a woman and a man went at it in the streets. And once the pigs showed up, folks got arrested first and questions were asked later.

Put My Name On It

Not wanting to make more of a scene than she already had, Natalia quickly turned on her heels facing Marcel again. "Say your peace. You have one minute."

"I only need twenty seconds." Standing before her, Marcel gently grabbed her hand. "Look, I know you don't believe me, but I swear to you, I didn't disappear. I was in jail. I'll explain the details to you later. Right now, I have something I want to ask you."

Pulling out a ring box with his other hand, he managed to open it and present it to her. A breath-taking platinum 6 carat round diamond solitaire engagement ring. "I planned on doing this a better way, but you left me no choice." Getting down on one knee he asked her in front of everyone, "Natalia will you marry me?"

In total shock, she gasped. She wondered what she should do. Never in a million years did she think Marcel would return. Not only did he come back, but he came back flashing a luxurious ring. It had to cost a grip because the custom design was outrageous.

Her eyes rose from the enticing diamond ring to Marcel's handsome face. Torn, she didn't know how to respond. Deep inside, she wanted to be his wife, but so much had gone down between them. A ring couldn't patch up their broken relationship. The hurt. The pain. The lies. The time that lapsed. How did she know he wouldn't disappear again?

"Say yes, please," Marcel begged while the crowd looked on in anticipation, waiting for Natalia's response. "I know you have doubts. And that's ok. Just know that I don't want nobody else but you. I've wanted you since I laid eyes on you. I need you in my life."

Natalia sighed, fighting back tears. Marcel was breaking her down. This is all she ever wanted—to be a wife and a mother.

"Keep it real, I know you feel the same way," he said sincerely.

"Say yes, hunni," a woman in the crowd yelled out. "He's a keeper."

"If you don't want him, I do," a young chick hollered. "He is fine."

"I'll take the ring," another young chick said. "Forget her. I'll be your wife, sexy."

"Stop being selfish," said an older lady standing by the pharmacy next door. "Think about your unborn child. Ain't that why you at the clinic in the first place?"

Marcel felt like Natalia was on the fence so he went in for the kill, pleading his case. "I want our family to be whole. Something I didn't have. Something you missed out on. Me, you, the twins, and the new baby, all under one roof." He gave her hand a soft kiss. "Please, Natalia, give us another chance. Let me prove it to you."

Natalia took a deep breath. She closed her eyes and formed her lips to say no. There's no way her heart could do this again. Opening her mouth, she shocked herself when she said, "Yes."

"Yes?" Marcel repeated. He needed to make sure that's what she said.

A smile formed on her lips when she realized that she accepted his proposal. "Yes! I'll marry you."

Marcel silently rejoiced while slipping the ring on her finger. He stood to his feet, wiping away her tears. "Don't cry. Everything's going to be alright."

Happy that things worked out, he took her into his arms. "I missed you so much. You just don't know."

"I missed you too. I hated being without you."

"That will never happen again."

The crowd cheered as they stood in front of the clinic kissing.

You won't regret saying yes."

Natalia's smiled bright. "I better not."

Marcel smiled back. "You won't. I plan to be the best husband and father ever."

Natalia punched him in the arm. "I'm still pissed at you for getting me pregnant again."

He smirked. "What can I say? Angry sex is the best sex."

"Whatever. You just nasty."

"You liked it."

Natalia playfully hit him again. "Don't tell me what I like."

Princess Diamond

Marcel scooped her up, carrying her in his arms to the car. "Let's go somewhere and celebrate. Where do you want to go?"

"I don't care as long as I'm with you."

Chapter 24

They kissed one more time before he put her down. He forgot he couldn't open the passenger's side door.

"See, you parked too damn close," Natalia said, climbing over the driver's seat. "When you get this?" she asked referring to his new whip.

"My lawyer got it for me while I was locked up. I had to switch out the other one. A convict not too far from your house owned the same make and model. That's how I got arrested. I left your house that night and they thought I was that nicca."

Natalia's eyes widened. "So, you were really in jail?"

"Hell yeah! What you thought I made that shit up? I wouldn't lie about being locked up."

"True. Come to think about it, I don't know nobody that would lie about it." Natalia sighed. "What about my car? I can't just leave it. It'll be towed"

"It should be. It's a piece of junk. Besides, I'm buying you a new one. My wife can't be rockin no raggedy shit like that. You deserve the best of everything."

My wife. Hmmmm. I like how that sounds. Natalia leaned over pecking her future husband's lips before resting her head on his shoulder. No matter how much she denied her feelings before, she couldn't deny them now. He meant the world to her. "So when's the wedding date?"

"Whenever you want it to be." Marcel cautiously looked around. "Let's get the hell outta here. Cause I can feel something is about to go down. I'm sure the jakes are on their way. Dude probably called them when he walked his punk ass away." Taking the blinkers off, Marcel took a quick look over his shoulder before proceeding into traffic.

Sure enough when they got down the block, Marcel saw the familiar red and blue flashing lights.

"Told you," he said to Natalia as she strained her neck to look out the back window.

The police arrived at the clinic ready to handle the domestic disturbance call they received.

Marcel rubbed Natalia's thigh before calmly making a right. There was distance between them and law and he intended to put even more miles between them driving as far away from the abortion clinic as he possibly could.

"Were you really going to get rid of my baby?"

Natalia raised her head off his shoulder. "That's a stupid question."

"Just for that we're having six kids."

"You's a damn lie."

Marcel chuckled. "Ok, maybe not six, but I do want another baby after this one. Then we can quit."

"Please. I'm getting my tubes tied after this baby."

"See, that's not fair."

"Ok. Maybe I won't go to that extreme. But I'm taking birth control."

Not if I can help it, Marcel thought. *I'll flush it all down the toilet.*

Natalia looked over at him, seeing the grin plastered on his face. "What you smiling so hard about?"

Marcel kept on smiling as he drove. "Nothing."

Except From Hott Girlz

Chapter 1

Pashion

Gary, Indiana

Back in the late 90's

"You know I'm sick and tired of coming up here about your hot ass," my mother said. "I can't keep coming up to school about you, missing work and shit. I'ma fuck around and get fired messing around with you and your bullshit."

I was forever getting into trouble at school. My mother was fed up with it. She had an attitude with me because she had to leave from work again for another parent-teacher conference with Mr. Preston.

Princess Diamond

My mother puffed on her cigarette as she drove like a bat out of hell. "You need to get your act together or you're going to find yourself in a world of trouble, Ms. Thang. Life is not as easy as you think it is. In the real world, you can't do and say anything you want. There are consequences for every decision you make. Your ass is going to learn the hard way. You think you know everything. Can't nobody tell you shit. Keep it up. You're going to fuck around and be in a ditch somewhere."

What was she talking about? I sat in the passenger's seat of my mother's Mercedes, rolling my eyes and sucking my teeth as she continued to vent. I was so damn sick of hearing her complain about my behavior. Every time I thought she was going to shut her big mouth, she opened it again. I wasn't trying to hear all that hot air she was blowing. If she had listened to my side of the story instead of taking the teacher's side every damn time, she would have known that it wasn't my fault. I didn't do anything.

Mr. Preston had been picking on me since the first day of class. He constantly found reasons to keep me after class, giving me bad grades so I'd have to stay after. He made up all kinds of phony excuses so that I got detention. During my confinement, all he did was stare at my long legs.

One day I got so mad that I cussed his ass out, kicked my desk over, and stormed the fuck out. He tried to stop me and I cussed his ass out again. I didn't belong in detention anyway. He claimed that I was late when I wasn't. I was in class walking to my seat when the tardy bell rang.

The next day when I came to school, I found out I'd been suspended for being disruptive in his class. My mother had to come to school about the matter. That was some bullshit. Just like today's incident was some bullshit. Secretly, Mr. Preston was a pervert. He wanted to fuck his students. I found out why he picked on me so much when he asked me to stay after class yesterday.

"Ms. Brooks, I want to talk to you about the rumors that I've been hearing," Mr. Preston began.

"And what is that?" I asked. I knew exactly what he was talking about, but I wanted his nasty ass to say it.

He looked at my cleavage before he spoke again, "Well, I've heard a few of my male students talking about the reputation that you and your friends have."

"And? You can't believe everything you hear, Mr. Preston. As a teacher, you should know that." I wanted to add, with your nasty ass.

Tiny beads of sweat appeared on his forehead as he continued to stare at my breasts. "Yes, you are right, but I've heard it several times. If everyone is saying it, it has to be true." He looked into my eyes briefly before he looked at my chest again. "Especially, if you are rumored to be having sex with older men."

Older men? This guy was really psycho. No boys in this school said that. They said a lot of things about my girls and me, but having sex with older men wasn't one of them. What he meant to say was he wanted to fuck me, but he didn't have the balls to say it.

"This is a waste of my time," I told him, picking up my books about to leave.

Before I could walk away, he grabbed me by my arm and pulled me into him. "Don't walk away from me when I'm talking to you, young lady."

He was standing so close to me that I could feel his hard-on. Then, he leaned in and tried to kiss me.

"Let me go," I told him, jerking away. "You's a trifling muthafucka. You don't care about no rumors. You just want me to stay after so you can try to get in my panties."

Mr. Preston looked nervous when I said that. "Now, Miss Brooks, you have obviously gotten the wrong impression. I'm trying to help you."

"Help me?" I said, getting madder by the second. "That's a new one. I guess you called yourself helping me by staring at my chest all day."

"You're out of line, Miss Brooks. I think I'm going to have to call your mother again," he threatened.

"I don't give a damn what you do," I told him while leaving. "I'll be glad to get suspended this time. Then, I won't have to see your triflin' face no more."

"Are you listening to me?" my mother asked, continuing to scold me.

Put My Name On It

I had no idea that my mind had drifted back to what happened between me and Mr. Preston. "Yes," I snapped. "I heard you."

"You'll see what I'm talking about soon enough. All you think about is your friends, designer clothes, and boys. Life has more meaning than that. You're just fast, but life is going to slow you down real soon."

I heard about all I could hear from her. "Ma, you don't know what I'm going through. All you're concerned with is work. You don't have a clue about what's going on with me."

"Look, I'm not going to make no excuses for my career," she replied.

My mother turned down our street, which was the same street and the same house in which she grew up.

She sighed. "How do you think these bills get paid? They sure as hell don't pay themselves. Money don't grow on trees."

"Well, I guess Neal must be a bill because you work on him on your off days too," I said, referring to all the sex that they had.

I heard them going at it, day and night.

"What did you just say?" my mother said as if she couldn't believe her ears. "I know you didn't say what I think you did."

I wanted to say more, but I didn't feel like arguing with her. I just wanted her to get off my back about Mr. Preston.

Princess Diamond

"You must've lost your damn mind, talking to me like that. What I do in my gawddamn house is my damn business. I'm the queen of this damn castle," she said adamantly.

I folded my arms across my chest with an attitude to match. "Humph. My grandma was the real queen of this damn castle—not you. You didn't raise me, she did. You ran out while she stayed behind handling your responsibility," I shot back.

Before I knew it, my mother had reached over and slapped me. She'd hit me so hard that my head hit the window.

"Don't you ever say no shit like that to me. Your grandmother might have raised you, but you're still my child. You will respect me no matter what," she cautioned. My mother whipped into our driveway. "I did what I had to do for us, and I'm damn proud of it. You wouldn't have none of those nice things you like if I didn't handle my business. I bought all those things for you, not your grandma. I was the one who worked day and night, long hours of overtime to make sure you had everything you ever wanted. So, don't you ever tell me what I did or didn't do, ungrateful ass bitch!" she screamed at me.

I held my face with my head down, not believing a word she'd said. "Well, that's not what grandma said. She said you left me behind because you were involved with a married man who used you up. He dumped you when you got pregnant with me."

Put My Name On It

My mother tried to hit me again, but I blocked her blow.

"I was going to be easy on your smart ass, but after what you just said, you can add another month to your punishment. Now, think about that, since you got smart ass shit to say," she said.

"What?" I yelled in shock. "You got to be kidding me. I won't be able to do nothing until Thanksgiving."

All I could think about was missing out on fun with the Hott Girlz.

"Just watch and see if I'm kidding," my mother spat. "You're going to stay on punishment until you change that funky attitude of yours or die trying, whichever comes first."

I was so pissed at my mother that I jumped out of her car before she could say another word, slamming the door hard.

I hated her ass.

Read Hott Girlz Available Now on Amazon!

www.ingramcontent.com/pod-product-compliance
Lightning Source LLC
Chambersburg PA
CBHW060817120626
46557CB00001B/252